"The death-throes of a colonial ___ ___se, punctuated by images of stran__ ___ ___he river of dead fish. One thinks at ___ ___ordimer, but Kitamura is very much her o\ ___ makes you feel keenly the tragedy of her three lost souls."

—Salman Rushdie

"I have been in a daze ever since I finished this book. *Gone to the Forest* is superb. It is so beautifully written, so balanced—there isn't a spare sentence or word in the whole thing. Utterly distinctive, it is almost allegorical in its force. Kitamura is one of the best living writers I've read, and she gives the dead ones a run for their money."

—Evie Wyld, author of *After the Fire a Still Small Voice*

"Katie Kitamura is a major talent. It is not often I read a book of controlled, illuminating prose and it is even more rare that the story therein survives the style. I was reminded of the writings of Herta Müller and J. M. Coetzee, both important storytellers of our time and vanguards of form. Kitamura's spare, elegant and affecting work in *Gone to the Forest* brings the reader in and out of the nexus of three souls caught in a nameless land, in a nameless time, and gently observes as they try to give name to their relation to one another, to the land, to the times and to themselves. *Gone to the Forest* is a book of atmospheres and moods, details and desires and Kitamura handles the nuances with the grace and confidence of a writer beyond her years."

—Laleh Khadivi, author of *The Age of Orphans*

"*Gone to the Forest* is a stark, urgent, beautiful novel. Katie Kitamura merges history and fable to create an explosive narrative about people trapped by terrible events they cannot control, but in which they are also deeply implicated. Its themes are ambitious—guilt and innocence, power and submission, meaning and nonsense. The characters and images of *Gone to the Forest* continue to haunt me, a tribute to their lasting emotional power and their creator's extraordinary gifts."

—Siri Hustvedt, author of *The Summer Without Men*

Praise for *The Longshot*

"In her debut novel, *The Longshot*, Katie Kitamura delivers the reader into the exotic, bruising, and hypermasculine world of mixed martial arts with startling economy and even more startling insight. . . . One lesson of *The Longshot* is you must fulfill your commitments, if only to find out what you're made of. Another is that Kitamura is a major talent."

—*Boston Globe*

"If you're planning to get into the ring with the heavyweights of boxing lit (A. J. Liebling's *The Sweet Science*, Leonard Gardner's *Fat City*), you need a knockout hook. Katie Kitamura, in her debut novel, has one."

—*Entertainment Weekly*

"Katie Kitamura has produced a lean, taut little novel as authentic as any sport could hope to have represent it. *The Longshot*, her debut effort, reads the way we imagine the best fighters to be: quiet, measured, self-assured, always thinking ahead . . . [with] a fierce sense of elegance."

—*The Daily Beast*

"Kitamura's descriptions of mixed-martial-arts fighting are brutal yet beautiful. . . . Her writing is spellbinding. . . . Kitamura is a genuine discovery."

—*Booklist*, starred review

"Spare and beautifully written. . . . [Kitamura] brings a physicality to her story with descriptions of the action so vivid the reader feels the pain of every punch and kick."

—*Publishers Weekly*

"A real shot to the heart—a resonant portrait of a man out to prove he can take anything the world throws at him."

—*Kirkus*

"Kitamura captures the intimacy shared by the men at battle. . . . Her crisp prose is well suited to describing combat, its staccato sentences delivered like the jabs and kicks of the fighters themselves. . . . Subtly revealing."

—*Times Literary Supplement*

"A rigorous fictional account that examines the sport, exploring themes of discipline and male-bonding."

—*Metro*, Book Pick (Canada)

"Kitamura, a young writer and art journalist, crafts her beautifully sparse words and pointed language to highlight a story of kinship, male bonding, and staying true to oneself."

—*The Last Magazine*

"Hemingway's returned to life—and this time, he's a woman."

—Tom McCarthy, author of *Remainder*

"Back in the day, we'd have wondered how a woman—a woman!—could know so much about this brutally masculine world. The marvel today is that Katie Kitamura can write about it with such grace, compassion, and breezy confidence. She knows her way around the ring and the human heart."

—Elizabeth Benedict, author of *The Practice of Deceit*

"Katie Kitamura has written a novel as terse, elegant, thoughtful and economical as Roy Jones, Jr., on his best days. Her writing is spare and graceful, her ear for dialogue precise, and she writes with the kind of controlled, compressed passion that produces literary gems."

—Jon Fasman, author of *The Geographer's Library*

"Deft, subtle and hard-hitting all at once. . . . A disquisition on hope, hurt and vulnerability that's heartbreakingly acute . . . Katie Kitamura has conjured a style that is spare, elegant and controlled; deadly in its scrutinizing gaze. . . . I am knocked out."

—Ekow Eshun, author of *Black Gold of the Sun*

"With refreshingly unadorned prose, Kitamura reduces to an intensely crystalline moment the tension surrounding a fighter and his coach as they prepare for a match. Kitamura's language sticks to the page with a delightful monocular clarity that invites readers to enter into the minds of these two men. *The Longshot* gives readers a rare glimpse into an intriguing world."

—Yannick Murphy, author of *Signed, Mata Hari*

"A terrific debut: charged, intimate, raw. Here is an author who not only understands the alloying of muscle and mentality in sport, the elation and heartbreak of competition, and of life, but can also write about it all with compassion and beautiful austerity."

—Sarah Hall, author of *The Electric Michelangelo*

gone to the forest

KATIE KITAMURA is based in New York and London. She has written for numerous publications, including *The New York Times*, *Wired* and the *Guardian*, and is a regular contributor to *Frieze*. She was a finalist in the 2010 New York Public Library Young Lions Fiction Award for her debut novel, *The Longshot*.

Also by Katie Kitamura

The Longshot

gone
to the
forest

a novel

katie kitamura

THE CLERKENWELL PRESS

First published in Great Britain in 2013 by
THE CLERKENWELL PRESS
An imprint of Profile Books Ltd
3A Exmouth House
Pine Street
London ECIR OJH
www.profilebooks.com

First published in the United States of America in 2012 by
Free Press, an imprint of Simon and Schuster Inc.

1 3 5 7 9 10 8 6 4 2

Printed and bound by
CPI Group (UK) Ltd, Croydon, CR0 4YY

A CIP catalogue record for this book is available from the British Library.

ISBN 978 1 84668 923 9
eISBN 978 1 84765 907 1

The paper this book is printed on is certified by the © 1996 Forest Stewardship Council A.C.
(FSC). It is ancient-forest friendly. The printer holds FSC chain of custody SGS-COC-2061

For Hari

I have gone to the forest.

—KNUT HAMSUN

part one
The Mountain

1

Tom hears the noise from across the hall. A quick stream of native patois. At first he thinks it is the servants talking. But then he hears the crackle of static. The high cadence of a bugle. The voice picks up again and is louder. Agitated and declaiming.

It is the radio—somebody has left the radio on. Tom gets to his feet. The old man is not in his study, he is out by the river. But the noise is not coming from the old man's study. Tom follows the sound down the corridor. He goes to the kitchen, thinking perhaps Celeste has been listening to the afternoon drama—

The kitchen is empty. The dishes sit washed and gleaming on the shelves. A drip of water from the tap. Perplexed, Tom turns around. The voice continues to speak from somewhere behind him. He follows the sound to the veranda. There, a radio sits on the edge of the table, the volume turned high.

Brothers, our time has come. We are tired of being ground under the boot of the white oppressor. We are tired of being suffocated by these parasites. For so many years we have not even been aware of their tyranny. We have been sleeping!

A chair has been pulled up to the table. As if someone has been sitting and listening intently. Tom does not immediately recognize the radio—he thinks it has been taken from the library, he cannot be sure. On the farm, they do not often listen to the wireless. Impossible to understand why it is here on the veranda.

Now it is time for us to awaken from our slumber. Rouse up, brothers! We will achieve our liberation and we will free this land! There will be a price. The parasites will not give up this country so easily. But we are brave, we are righteous men—

Tom frowns and switches the radio off. It is unusual to hear a native voice on the radio. The patois is thick and filled with anger. He can barely understand the words, it is a guttural nonsense to his ears. He still cannot imagine who could have moved the radio to the veranda. No servant would have dared do such a thing.

He looks at the chair. He thinks he can see an indentation in the seat. Like a ghost has broken into the farm, and in broad daylight, too. It is a good thing he was the one to discover it. Tom looks both ways before adjusting the chair and picking up the radio. Holding the machine, he looks out onto the land. It is quiet and he retreats inside.

THE HOUSE SITS by the edge of the river. It is big—a house with multiple wings and rooms and a veranda running along three sides. Outside this giant house there is a double row of trees, planted by the old man's natives. Tom sits in the dirt beneath one of these trees, where there is shade from the blistering sun.

Tom's father was among the first of the white settlers. Forty years ago, the old man arrived in the country and claimed his piece of land. One hundred thousand acres down a ten-mile spine running through the valley. The land belonged to no one and then it belonged to him. A stake driven into the soil. The old man swallowed up the land and filled it with native hands. The money and good fortune came shortly after.

The farm sits adjacent to the border and from its perimeter the neighboring country is visible. The parcel is big and the soil arable and there is also the river, which is wide and fast, clouded with sediment and Sargasso weed. The old man picked the land for the river. It runs straight out to the sea. The carnivorous dorado swim through in herds and purple hyacinth sprout on the surface.

For many years, the old man used the land as a cattle farm. The vast acreage turned to pasture, the herd growing by the year. A small crop also harvested. Today, he runs the farm as a fishing resort, for tourists who come from all parts of the world. The old man is imperious with the guests in the same way he is imperious with his servants. They do not seem to mind. They stay in the guest wing of the house and pay good money for the privilege.

Tom manages the farm. He oversees the daily operation of the cattle pasture, the fields, the river and the house. It is a great deal for one man to handle but Tom is good at his job. He is good with the fluctuations of the land, which he is able to read correctly. Also the domestic affairs of the house and kitchen. Tom is diligent and has an eye for detail, in which he often takes comfort.

Tom is the old man's first and only son. This means that one day he will inherit the farm. He will run the fishing resort and that will be the whole of his life. Tom can see no other kind of future. It is the only horizon before him, but he has no sense of its constriction. Tom has a passion for the land. It is the one thing he knows intimately. He burrows into it, head down in the dirt, and cannot imagine a life beyond it.

Therefore, Tom sits beneath his tree. He presses his limbs into the soil, as if they would grow roots. It is the last week of the season but it is still hot. Normally, the tourists would have stayed. For the sun and the fishing, and with winter so slow to come. They would have sat on the veranda in friendly clusters, ideal for souvenir photographs. The women in tea dresses and the men in linen suits. Drinks served on the veranda after a hot day on the river.

Instead, the veranda is empty and silent. The radio having been returned to the library and the chair righted. Tom looks up when the door opens. The old man steps out onto the veranda. He is still in his work clothes, having spent the afternoon shooting old livestock. It is a task he always does himself. There are traces of gunpowder on his boots, the smell of fresh blood. The old man stands on the veranda, six feet tall in his riding boots, and does nothing to acknowledge his son.

After a long silence, he calls to him.

"Thomas."

He is called Tom by everyone except his father, who calls him Thomas. It causes a split inside Tom/Thomas. He thinks of himself as Tom but only recognizes himself as Thomas. He does not know his own name. He realizes, has been aware for some time, that this is no way for a man to be. It is not something he can discuss with his father. He rises to his feet and goes to the old man.

"Yes, Father."

His father watches him and is silent. He looks at Tom like he has never seen him before in his life. Possibly he wishes it were so. All this land and they cannot get away from each other, though that is not the way Tom sees it. The sun glows orange in the sky. For a long time his father is silent. Then he speaks.

"The Wallaces dine with us tonight."

"Yes."

"Have you spoken to Celeste?"

"Yes."

"Fine."

The old man nods. On the farm they squander money on food. The youngest animals are slaughtered for the table. Pods stripped from the stalk. Roots upended from the soil. And then there are the tins of foie gras and caviar, the cases of wine that are flown in from abroad. Everything for the kitchen. Anything that could be needed.

Tom turns to go. He is not more than five paces away when

something makes him stop. He is already turning when his father calls him again. Tom waits, some distance from his father.

"What is Celeste serving?"

"Tonight?"

His father ignores the question. Tom is immediately uneasy. It is not a normal query. The old man treats Tom like his chief of staff. He manages for the old man, sometimes he allows himself to imagine he is indispensable to him. But he is never able to get used to the idea. There is never the opportunity. The old man does not allow for it.

For example, now. His father is a man of appetite. He trusts Celeste with his stomach and that makes Celeste the most trusted member of the household. But now his father is asking what the menu will be and this is not normal. Fortunately, Tom has discussed the meal with Celeste. He clears his throat—a habit the old man hates—and begins.

"Oysters. Gnocchi. Lamb. Salad. Then cheese and ice cream."

His father nods.

"The oysters?"

"They were brought in this morning."

His father nods again.

"No fish?"

"No."

"Why no fish?"

"I will ask Celeste."

"Tell her to put out the last of the caviar. I have no need of it. And tell Celeste to set the table for five."

Mr. and Mrs. Wallace are occasional friends. They are marginal people of no interest to his father. The old man has made that abundantly clear. He does not say who the fifth guest is. Tom waits. The old man looks up.

"Do you have something else to tell me?"

He thinks of the radio on the veranda. Who left it there? Tom shakes his head. No. Nothing. His father nods and Tom goes. He walks to the kitchen to look for Celeste. This time she is there, stuffing pastry for the farmhands. She palms the meat into the pastry and slaps the food down on the tray. He stares at the meat. It is pink and red and white. Raw and unformed. Celeste looks up.

"He wants to know if there is fish for tonight."

She shakes her head.

"Ah no."

"He would like fish."

She sighs and wipes her hands on a tea towel.

"Why?"

He ignores the question.

"Also he says to serve caviar to start, and to set the table for five."

She shakes her head. *Tcha tcha tcha,* her tongue in her mouth. She throws down the tea towel. Neither Tom nor Celeste wants to serve fish at supper. But both know there will now be fish alongside the lamb, an additional course in an already long meal. Celeste will dress the fish in saffron and butter. Jose will pass around the table with the platter resting on his arm, lifting slabs of fish to the plates. He will use the silver serving spoon to pool sauce on top. Tom clears his throat.

"Did you take the radio out to the veranda?"

She stares at him blankly.

"What do you mean?"

Tom nods, then leaves the kitchen and walks outside. The air is still. He stands outside the house.

Something is wrong. The tourist season has been a failure. It was supposed to refill the coffers. It was meant to provide security. But the season brought them nothing and now the money is running out. Everybody knows the money is running out. It is no longer secret, it can be seen everywhere on the farm.

But there will be caviar, and guests! He does not understand his father. He goes up the steps and into the house. He walks along the veranda, along the perimeter of the house. Everything is as it should be. He enters the dining room. The table has not been set. Five, the old man said to lay the table for five. Tom stands for a long moment. He looks at the heavy oak table and the chairs. He stares at the marble topped credenza.

TOM RETURNS TO the row of trees. He sits in idleness. It is the tempo of this place. It overtakes him, he has no resistance to it. It is true Tom is a good manager, but that is almost despite himself, fundamentally he is lazy. His father is different. His mother was different. His mother was like his father, she was not from this place. She was nervous, set to a tempo that was out of pace with the draw of the land.

It could not be changed. His mother came ten years after his father and left ten years ago, dead from exhaustion. They shipped her body back across the sea in a bare pine box at the request of her family. The life had been too much for her. His father said that the moment she set foot on the land. Nobody was surprised when she died. It took her twenty years to do it and they were surprised it took her so long. She had been dying the whole time. She was half dead when she gave birth to him and after that died by increments.

Tom remembered her sometimes. Early on she had been diagnosed consumptive. That was a disease from long ago, an illness that no longer existed, but it still managed to kill her. She ate up her body. In the last years of her life she burned through her organs and limbs, she combusted inside her skin. Like she was in a hurry and couldn't wait any more. Sometimes he could smell the scent of her decay, lifting high off her body.

That was his mother. She gave birth to him and he slithered from between her legs and out into the land and dust. From the start he was of this place. He was country born and at home with the bramble. For the first year Celeste nursed him at her tit. She held him while he scratched and suckled. Celeste had a son exactly Tom's age, Jose. She raised the two boys together. Jose's father being nowhere in sight. However, the two boys did not grow up like brothers.

Jose was healthy, indefatigable, stubborn even as an infant.

Tom, on the other hand, was not a strong child. He had a skin condition that weakened his body and stunted his growth. Dry scales grew at his elbows and knees. Left alone, Tom would peel long strips of skin from his body. When Celeste discovered the raw lengths she would take him to the river and press handfuls of mud against his wounds. Covered in river sludge, he was left out in the sun to heal.

Between themselves, the natives called him Lizard Boy. His father blamed his mother for the boy's condition but Tom always believed the weakness to be his own. In the same way the land was seated deep inside him: it was a congenital disorder of sorts. He also knew the weakness meant that he would not die like his mother. It was self-preserving. He retreated into his weakness and lay down inside it. It was a thing of comfort in a life that was not, on the whole, filled with comfort.

As a child he sought solace in lies, and has been a liar ever since. He is not a good liar but he is a persistent one. The first time he lied over a plate. Tom had been sent to the neighboring farm for the afternoon. The farmer's son had a set of plastic dishes. The colors were cheap and bright and when Tom pressed his thumbnail into the plastic it left a crescent-shaped mark. Tom wanted one of the plates. He slipped it into his pocket. Then he got up quickly and left without saying goodbye.

His father was waiting for him at the steps of the house, like he had seen his guilt from a distance. He stopped Tom and lifted him from the ground, his fingers digging into Tom's armpits in a way that was not friendly. Tom kicked to be lowered and the plate fell to the floor. The plastic sounded ugly and hollow against the tile. Stupidly, he tried to conceal the plate with the sole of his boot.

His father did not look surprised.

"Where is that from?"

"The boy gave it to me."

"He gave it to you?"

"A gift."

"The boy gave you a gift."

"Yes."

"You are lying."

He was whipped by a servant. His father did not bother to listen. To the whizz of the cane, to his miserable shrieks and howls. Nonetheless, Tom continued to lie. His father asked him who broke the vase in the hall. Who left the gate open and set loose the cattle. It was like the sight of his father's face made the lie that followed inevitable.

Even then, all Tom wanted was the old man's approval. Unfortunately, he was never able to act in a manner to win it. Tom knew he would not be punished for the act itself, only for the lie. What his father did not understand was the lying. He needed, on the whole, to dominate what he did not understand. Tom told one lie and then another. He was whipped by the servants again.

TOM WAS NOT a good liar, but Tom's mother had been good enough to make a career of it. She lied to her husband for the full course of her affair with a neighboring farmer. She used Tom as an excuse. She said he was uncomfortable with himself and other children. He needed to be socialized—that was the fashionable term she applied to her son's unfashionable condition. Every other day she walked him three miles to the neighboring estate. She left him in the yard with the other children and disappeared inside.

The children played in the dirt and listened to the shrieks that rang out across the farmstead. Which sometimes sounded like an animal dying, painfully. She came out of the farmhouse with her skin a hectic red and one hand pressed against her head. Tom watched as she smoothed her hair into place. Calmed the surface of her dress. Then they walked the three miles home, his hand sticky in hers. He knew but did not mind the fact that she was lying. He thought the secret would bring them closer.

There were other flaws in his character, beyond dishonesty and misapprehension, which together conspired to make the son incomprehensible to the father. For example, Tom was a coward. He was easily frightened and physically uncertain. He was not very old when the physical fear became a moral one. It was therefore natural that his father held him in contempt: the old man does not recognize fear as a valid emotion.

It did not help that Tom was especially afraid of the dorado. To him they were a terrifying fish. The dorado grew four feet long in the river, larger than a child and much larger than the child Tom had been. The male fish bore square blocked foreheads and male and female alike their bodies turned gray as they died out of water. But while alive the fish were fearless and had tremendous appetite.

Tom's father loved the dorado. He is this fish: his father is the dorado. Once, when Tom was a boy, he took him out on the river. He might have been experimenting with the idea of being a father because he was unusually patient. He taught Tom to cast out to the water. He showed him how to reel in. He said very little but he told him that the dorado were a vicious fish that ate into a man's strength.

Tom remembered how his father caught the dorado on the line. How he began to reel it in. The fish rose out of the water and dropped back in. It appeared to Tom as large as a grown man, as large as his father. It jerked through the water, under the boat, into the air, back into the water. The rod almost bending in two. Tom was not certain that his father would bring it in. He thought surely the rod would snap.

But his father brought the fish in. It was a giant. Male, with the alien crested forehead, the yellow body thrashing against the line. His father lifted it high in the air. He admired the heft and weight, the golden turn of the scales, the tremendous girth of the fish. Then he placed it in Tom's arms. Tom almost fell with the weight of the dorado, the coldness of the scales, the inner muscle of the animal shuddering hard against its death.

When he came to, his father was standing above him, holding the fish by its tail. Tom watched as he seized a knife and dug into the belly of the fish. He drew a long vertical slit and the crimson guts of the animal tumbled out onto the deck. He ignored his son as he scooped the intestines into one hand

and threw them back into the river. The dorado swarmed the boat, jaws snapping.

The fish became their livelihood. Running a farm was an expensive business. The river supported the farm and allowed them to maintain the large holding of land. More and more tourists came to the province in search of the mighty dorado. His father took them out on the boats at dawn. He taught them to cast out and reel in. He brought in the fish and gutted them before their eyes, he treated them the same way he had treated Tom, years ago.

When his father arrived in the country he was a young man. Now he is old. Now he sits—he squats, he straddles—the land. But his presence has been heavy from the start. He picked out the land by riding in the night with a torch held high above his head. A native dug a trench in the soil behind him. The next day they went back with wood and wire and it was done. The old man makes his choice. He grips it out of the air with his hands. He is essentially a violent man.

Tom is different. He does not force himself upon the land. He does not force himself upon anything. There is very little that Tom can call his own. Tom is not like his father, Tom has chosen nothing. He did not choose the country or the piece of land. He did not choose the business of the farm. He did not choose the house, with its dark rooms and corridors. All this was chosen for him, and Tom barely aware of it. It is simply his world.

FOR SEVERAL YEARS the pool of guests has been dwindling. There have been empty rooms at high season and the river has remained full of fish, something impossible even a few years ago. Across the province there are fewer visitors. They are far from the cities to the north. The cost of travel is high. And there is unrest in the country, Tom has heard it said. It is growing and the news of it is spreading abroad—bad stories, violent stories that do not inspire confidence.

One by one the gentleman farmers are moving. The idea of living in open land surrounded by natives is no longer appealing. Those with houses in the cities are giving up the country life and moving north. They are closing their farms and estates, which are becoming too hard to protect, having always been vast and exposed. They leave them in the hands of the hardier settlers who remain in the province and are a restless and violent presence. They do not say when they might return.

The circle of refined company is shrinking day by day. Once there were dances and banyan parties—once there was a social calendar! Tom and his father remain. His father does not believe in the city. The other farmers tell him to move out of the country, that it is dying in front of them, that soon it will no longer be safe. His father chooses to stay on the side of the land. He cannot imagine being without the farm. In this, father and son are united.

It is now near evening. Tom stands in front of the mirror in his room. It is large and crowded with things. Furniture brought over from the old country by his mother or father. Objects shipped to them by strangers. He finds these histories oppressive but has essentially grown used to it. Tom does not expect privacy, even in his own room. Carefully, he adjusts the lapel on his jacket and smooths his hair back with grease. He checks the crease in his trousers and then leaves the room, closing the door behind him.

He walks the house in search of his father. He goes across the foyer, which is full of potted trees. Miniature orange trees. Plum trees. He passes the dining room and notes the good linen and silver and china. He sees that the table is now set for five. Five plates, five sets of glasses and cutlery. He pauses, and then walks out to the veranda, slowly.

He walks in the direction of the river and finds his father within minutes. The open land pulls to the river. Which has become the old man's sole preoccupation as the province empties and the tourism dwindles. A year ago they installed the river farm. Now the pools float in the middle of the river like space age contraptions. The fish birthing and growing, inside the skin of the device. The river flushing in and out.

Tom frowns as he looks at the river. The old man has staked much on the river farm. The pools were installed at vast expense and they sucked the savings—the bounty of those years of lush tourism, now coming to an end—right into the water. At first it did not seem promising. The natives talked of evil and contamination. The eggs floated in the steel and mesh like a river disease.

But then the fish grew. They grew until the pools were full of fish flesh, pressed close together. Now it seems clear that the river farm is what will allow them to live. It will sustain the farm, through the rumors of unrest. It will pay for the imported caviar, the cashmere blankets, the fur coats, the coffee and tea. His father jokes that he is become a fishmonger but already there are plans for more pools, placed downstream, placed upstream. The province empties of landlords and tourists but there are always the fish and the natives.

Every week they drag the pools out of the water and the fish are culled. Then they are sold to buyers in the cities. They are packed into ice and flash frozen and shipped around the world. It is ridiculous, but they are earning themselves a reputation. His father talks about sustainable models of growth. He says there will be money soon, in the next year.

Tom does not like the river farm. When he looks into the water it is like the river is choking on the pools. The pools hovering like prey amidst the hyacinth. Being of the country, he cannot wish to dominate it in the same way as his father. Who in some ways is still a visitor here. But Tom knows his father is right. Soon the river farm will be established. The money will flow in like water. The money is floating in the river now, and it will save them.

Which is why his father stands and stares at the water—the way a man stares at a pile of gold. Tom watches his father looking at the pools. The pools can only be seen by the clearsighted. They are nothing but the faintest trace in the water. The old man is dressed in dinner clothes. A rim of dust gathers around the toe of his shoe, is lifted on a slow gust of wind. The wind goes, and the dust is gone and the old man's feet stand in the dirt.

The sound of a motor vaults across the silence. His father looks up. Tom sees the Wallaces' Ford pulling across the land. A small cloud of dust follows as it kicks down the track. The dust pulls and tugs and puffs and grows behind the vehicle. The motor rumble comes closer. His father stands and watches as the car approaches. Tom has already turned and is walking back to the house. He turns his head once to look back. The car is inching closer across the horizon. Tom quickens his pace.

By the time the car has pulled through the gates of the house the servants are ready and the ice in the liquor trolley has been freshened. Tom stands in the shadow of the veranda and watches as the car pulls down the drive. His father stands at the foot of the steps, one hand slipped into his suit pocket. His face is expressionless. The driver pulls the door open. Mr. Wallace. Mrs. Wallace. A third figure steps out of the car. A young woman, in a brightly patterned dress, emerges from the interior.

2

The dorado is served in green sauce. It is served before the lamb and after the oysters and caviar. They sit around the table in silence as the wine is poured. The sun is setting and outside the sky continues to give off light. The dining room is open to the veranda but the room itself is half in darkness. Jose returns and lights the candles. His father nods to him and they listen to his footsteps as he goes. Then the room drops into silence again.

After a measurable pause—in which they sit and do not look at each other, and the candles waver and tremble in the silence—his father leans forward and picks up his wine glass. He takes a sip and examines the liquid hue. Mrs. Wallace looks at him. He almost looks benevolent, sitting in the candlelight with his wine glass in hand. Mrs. Wallace makes an attempt at conversation. (Mr. Wallace does not. Mr. Wallace knows better.)

"I have been saying to George, they must do something about this unrest amongst the natives. It is the Government's responsibility to take some kind of action."

The old man looks up from his glass of wine. He stares at Mrs. Wallace from across the table. Bravely, she continues.

"They should send in soldiers. They should teach them a lesson, before it gets out of hand. They are capable of anything, the natives. They are dangerous and cruel. It is impossible to reason with them. I wonder that they don't see that."

Mr. Wallace shakes his head.

"Enough, Martha."

The old man ignores them both. He lowers his wine glass and looks across the table at the girl.

When the girl stepped out of the car she was a thin ankle followed by a ruffled tea dress. Her hair set in waves. Her mouth carefully rouged. She looked lost in the dress and in the car, a pantomime of vulnerability. Tom sits beside her at the dinner table. His father sits across. Tom watches the girl. He has no idea how old she is. She looks like a child but he already knows she is no child.

He learns the facts about the girl. She is Mrs. Wallace's second cousin. She is twenty-nine and part French. She has won herself—through hard application, nothing coming easy in life—a questionable reputation. Although really there is no question about it at all, the meaning being clear to everyone. There was trouble at home and she was shipped to Mrs. Wallace, for a length of time unspecified. The meaning of that also being clear.

Mrs. Wallace does not know the girl but she is responsible for her. It is evident, they are in this together. She looks at the girl and her gaze is complicit. Tom thinks: being women the collusion comes to them naturally. He has heard it said before. Mrs. Wallace touches the girl on the wrist. She is careful but proprietary, proprietary but wary. She will be happy when the problem of the girl is solved and she will not miss her when she is gone.

For now she watches the girl. She measures up her assets and tests her strength in performance. Tom also watches the girl. She sits at the table. She speaks when she is spoken to. She is docile, she is polite. She is all this but there is nothing about her Tom trusts. He tells himself that she is not especially pretty. It is only her extreme pallor—she is so pale that when she blushes the color is hectic like a bruise—and her air of apparent youth that give the impression of attractiveness.

His father is a man of taste. The girl is nothing and yet—Tom watches his father watch the girl. The old man is still handsome. He is vain and vanity needs feeding. The women in the valley have been doing the feeding but the circle has been shrinking as one by one the farms close and the whites retreat to the city. Now there are not even the tourists to rely on.

This girl—sent out to Mrs. Wallace, small and pale and cunning—is perfectly shaped to capture the old man. She is nothing special but she is there and that is the difference. They are losing, have lost, the yardstick by which to measure the company of women. Not that Tom was ever a judge. He has not exactly been exposed to the female species.

Tom is filled with the urge to slap the girl across the face.

His own vehemence taking him by surprise. Tom's eyes stay on his father as he sips the wine and watches the girl.

"Carine."

The girl looks up at him and then blinks. She waits for him to speak. Mr. Wallace and Mrs. Wallace look up from their plates. Tom does not look up. He stares down at his plate. He has not touched the food apart from the oysters. Topped with vinegar and white pepper. He slurped them down one after the other. Now his appetite is gone. He prods the food in front of him but does not eat.

"Do you like the fish?"

His father's voice is slow and cajoling. The tone an offer, a proposition to the girl. Tom sees her find her terrain in the words. She and the old man look at each other. A transaction in their gazes and she opens herself up. Tom sees it happen: so the girl has aligned herself with the old man. Some intimacy has been established between them, in front of all of them, in that small and meaningless exchange.

The obscenity of it is not lost on anyone at the table. Mr. Wallace clears his throat and reaches for his wine glass. Mrs. Wallace looks down at her plate and pushes a chunk of fish with the tines of her fork. She toys with the fork and then sets it down without eating. Tom sees that they are ashamed. Of the trap that they have set, that is now in motion.

"Do you? Like the fish?"

Quickly, the girl reaches for her fork. She spears the flesh, breaking off a large piece and lifting it to her mouth. Her lips are pale and dry and cracked at the edges. It is the weather,

Tom thinks. She is not used to the dryness of this country. She edges her mouth around the meat and swallows it whole. Tom looks down at his plate and slashes the fish with his fork.

The table is silent. Tom can hear her chewing. The indelicate chomping of her teeth and the loud gulp when she swallows. She continues chewing as she reaches for her water glass. They sit and stare at the girl. She takes a long swallow of water to wash the food down. Then she looks directly at his father and smiles—smiles so the rims of her teeth, which are small and white, show between her lips.

"I like it."

He nods and smiles.

"Thomas caught the fish earlier today."

He looks at his son. She follows the old man's gaze and turns to look at Tom. She is still smiling. There is nothing timid about her now. Her eyes are bold and jumping. He looks into them and the corners of her mouth turn further upward. Like she is amused. Confused, he glares at her then looks down at his plate and forks up a mouthful of fish.

"Thomas is a natural fisherman. It is in his blood."

Tom knows his father is making fun of him. The old man smiles at him. Tom nods and then looks away. It amuses the old man to mock his son in front of strangers. Not that Tom cares what Mr. Wallace and Mrs. Wallace and this girl think. He does not care in the least.

"Thomas is a young man of many abilities."

Now his father is looking at the girl. He is still smiling. The girl is watching him and despite all her wiles she is in danger of growing fascinated. Tom can already tell. His father is more than twice her age but her eyes are pinned to his lips as he speaks to her in his fur-lined baritone. The old man cheats wild horses of their freedom with this voice. It runs deep into his chest, silky smooth and dry.

Tom dislikes the girl and is fearful of her. But he does not want her to her fall into the old man's trap. Tom lives at the bottom of the trap. There is not very much space and he does not want to share his father with her. Tom has spent a lifetime watching people fall down the hole. He has never enjoyed the company. The girl looks at his father. She widens her eyes. It is too late, he thinks. She is already falling.

"Thomas can take you fishing some time. If you like."

"I would like."

She says the three words evenly and quickly. What she says—the *would* and the *like*—has nothing to do with fishing or with Tom or with anything that has been discussed at the table, anything that has been said out loud, since they arrived on the farm in their car.

Or perhaps it does. Have to do with everything that has happened since they arrived. Because now his father leans forward. His eyes rest on Tom and then return to the girl. He smiles. She smiles. The whole table smiles. Mr. Wallace and Mrs. Wallace sit back and for the first time that evening Mr. Wallace cracks a smile that is broad as daylight.

Only Tom does not smile. He glares at the dinner guests. They would do better to be cautious. They are beaming at his father—they grin and grin, mouths wide open—but they would do better to be aware of the situation they have walked into. Whatever that situation may be. The Wallaces are fools. They are no match for his father.

THE NEXT DAY Tom oversees the storage of the outdoor furniture. All summer the lawn and veranda are dotted with daybeds and settees. Today they gather the furniture from the lawn—the sign that the summer season is officially over. It is a full day's work. The servants bring the tables and chairs to the veranda. The wood needs oiling and there are necessary repairs.

Tom stands in the middle of the fray. He directs the servants. He inspects the polish. He checks the removal of the stains. His father stops to observe the proceedings. He brushes a hand against the wood. It has been made to order in the style of the furniture back in the old country. A reminder of the separation between the farm and the rest of the country, it is also the separation itself. The barrier being made of furniture and teapots. The old man nods approval and waves to the servants to continue. Then he motions for Tom to follow.

They walk around the veranda and out to the lawn. His father stops and looks in the direction of the servants on the veranda. They are bent over the furniture. Two men pick up a table and move in the direction of the storeroom.

"That's a good job."

Tom is pleased. It is true it is a good job. He has exerted

himself today, they all have. He notes that his father is in a good mood. Perhaps he slept well. The Wallaces left early, knowing better than to wear out their welcome. The farm is theirs again. Tom stands beside his father, in what he believes to be the glow of his approval.

The father invites the son to sit down. There are two chairs that have not been taken in, that stand forgotten in the middle of the lawn. Tom sits down. His father sits down next to him. He crosses his legs at the ankles. He folds his hands into a steeple and taps finger to knuckle. *Buh buh buh.* He sits and watches his son. He does not look out at the land. He does not look at the river, which is visible down the slope of land and through the trees. He looks at Tom.

"What do you think of Carine?"

Tom shrugs.

"She is pretty, no?"

Tom stares at his father. He cannot believe that his father can be serious about this girl and yet. And yet he is sitting here in this way, with his son, and he is telling him that he finds the girl pretty. He shakes his head. His father smiles and looks amused.

"No? Come, Thomas. You must admit that she is pretty."

He shrugs again.

"For a country boy you have high standards."

The old man pauses. Is watching him.

"Mrs. Wallace hoped you might take a fancy to the girl."

His father, still watching him. The realization dawns on Tom. The girl is intended for him. That was the purpose of the visit. The meaning of the looks that passed between the Wallaces and his father. He does not easily believe it—he approaches the idea cautiously, because it is not often that the father thinks of the son.

But what does he think of the girl? The thought of her returns abruptly and he does not know what he thinks. He thinks of her pale skin and her small sharp teeth and before he knows it the girl is settling inside his mind. Turning and making a home for herself there. He shakes his head.

"Soon you will be running the farm."

Tom looks up. His father has never said this, he has never put it into words. The promise has been understood but never actually stated. The date never articulated in terms such as *soon*. But now the old man has spoken the words and the difference is palpable, the difference is clear as daylight. Tom clears his throat. He tries to smile. He would like to thank his father but knows it would not be the thing. His father continues. More gently.

"You will. And when you do, a woman—"

He pauses, as if in consideration of his own past. He makes a minor correction.

"—a woman, of the right kind, will be a great help."

He wonders if his father believes that the girl is a woman of the right kind. A woman of the right kind, for a certain kind of thing. The thought of the girl returns to him like a flood and she kicks inside his brain.

"I told Mrs. Wallace that I thought you were not opposed to the idea."

29

He pauses.

"I thought that she liked you. Did you not?"

It has been decided. He hears the decision in his father's voice. It is almost a comfort. For a second he thought his father was asking. The idea of the girl and the idea of his choice—a choice, the choice of a woman—had spread through his body like a rash. Now the idea is gone and his body is restored to health. He nods and considers the slope of land running to the river. Soon to be his.

"Take her fishing."

A courting amongst the dorado—a terrible thought. Tom is now an excellent fisherman. On a good day he can outfish his father. He is slow and obstinate—good qualities in a fisherman. Whereas his father sees the sport as a contest of wills, a question of winning and domination. He is too easily drawn in. Tom only wants to capture the fish and bring it home and eat it.

It hardly matters. He is a good fisherman but he is still terrified of the fish. Everything about the animal is foreign to him. The gaping mouth and the razor sharp teeth—sharper than the teeth of any other animal, sharp in a way that has nothing to do with the necessities of the civilized world. The scales are so bright gold that he is sometimes blinded by the color of the fish, as in the brightness of the sun.

He will take her fishing. He will woo her on the river. His father has chosen. The old man watches him and then stands up and strides away. He does not say anything further. Tom sits and listens to the sound of his feet on the lawn. The lawn is empty and he hears the old man's steps longer than is natural. It is oppressive but there is a comfort in it. Tom does not like to be alone.

HE TAKES THE girl fishing and a week later they are engaged. He does not know how the engagement happens. One minute they are fishing and the next Mr. Wallace and Mrs. Wallace are standing with his father on the veranda. There are champagne bottles being opened, toasts being made, and in the middle of it the girl. She wears the ring his father gave him to give her. His mother's ring: the talisman of a failed contract.

Still, in the week since the engagement he has become painfully aware of the girl. Her presence brings on the migraine— he cannot think clearly, he needs to lie down. He thinks of her like this; he imagines stretching out beside her. He thinks he is in love with her. With this patch of land that will soon be his. It is small—a mere one foot by five feet and barely a hundred pounds—but it will be his, to do with as he likes. This plot of earth. That he will take to his bed as he likes, and keep close beside him.

A man feels a certain way toward his property. And Tom has never owned anything in his life. So he is in danger of being carried away, only he is a man both phlegmatic and wary. He does not know how to lose his head. He sees that the girl can look after herself. She lands on her feet like a cat dropped out a window. Being nimble in mind and body. But here she comes—she stands beside him, behind him, the fabric of her dress grazing his elbow, his hand, and it is hard not to feel what he feels. Her hair brushes against his shoulder and again he feels what he feels.

Although it has to be said. He can feel and feel away but the coupling, now official, is far from fully achieved. He has barely touched the girl. He is all too conscious of the fact. There was a churlish kiss—churlish on whose side? He hardly knows but suspects his own—in front of his father and the Wallaces. At the time of the champagne bottles and the toasts. And then very little since. He has touched her hand but not held it. Once he touched the small of her back.

She is cool and hard. Like marble or some other stone. He touches her neck and she leans back against the hand. Only for a second. The flesh is nonresponsive. It is like he is not even touching her, like his hand has been obliterated by her coldness. He puts his hand away. He admits that he does not know how to approach her. She is different from the others. Not that there have been any: Tom knows nothing about the ways of women.

It does not trouble him too much. There is enough time. There is all the time in the world! They will be married and then there will be many months, months and years and decades, in which to learn how best to approach the girl. He sees her like a piece of wild game. He is just circling and circling and taking his time. Eventually he will throw ropes around her neck and legs and yank her to the ground.

Meanwhile, the Wallaces are at the farm all the time, with all their civilization. They arrive in the afternoon for tea. They stay for dinner after tea. Lately the house is only empty in the morning. His father tolerates their company. He has found his son a mate. The change in routine is a small price to pay for it. Tom knows that his father does not like the Wallaces. Tom does not like them either. They sit on the chairs like they already belong to them, eyeing the silver, eating the food.

Checks are put into place. It will not do to let the Wallaces loose upon the farm. Mrs. Wallace goes so far as to ask Celeste to prepare a dish for supper. "The lamb we ate last week. Perhaps you could make it tonight?" As if she were already mistress of the house. The old man is obliged to send them away. The Wallaces do not come to the farm that day or the next. Nor does the girl. Tom becomes anxious without her. Finally his father telephones and orders them to send the girl to tea.

The girl comes alone. She has put on a fresh dress, bright yellow with a pattern of flowers. Hesitating, she steps onto the veranda and he comes forward to greet her. She says to him that she has already taken the dress in twice. She is shrinking, she is wasting away. It is the heat, she says. It is the food. She cannot find the food that she is used to here. She smiles at him and shrugs. He does not know what to say. It is true that her color is feverish. They are alone for the first time since they have been engaged.

Cautiously, she puts her hand on his arm. She is still smiling. He stares down at her and doesn't move. She tightens her grip. She begins to angle his body closer to hers. He thinks that is what she is doing—he isn't entirely sure. He feels panic. What does the girl want from him? What is it she expects? The panic grows and abruptly he shakes her hand off.

The girl does not look especially surprised. She smiles and looks away. With one hand she smooths the front of her dress. He watches her hand flutter down its surface. Up and then down again. Tom longs for his father, who would know what to do. The girl continues to brush at her lap, now frowning a little. She removes an invisible hair, dangles it from her fingers, drops it to the ground.

He says to her that he will go find his father. She is silent for a moment and then as he turns to go, she tells him not to. Her voice rises and then falters. She is asking him not to go. They stare at each other. She walks forward a little and then she places her hand on his chest. He stares down at the hand. Which is small and not particularly clean. Abruptly, he steps away.

"Can I get you something to drink?"

"Fine. Yes."

"What would you like?"

"Gin."

He nods and walks to the drinks trolley. Gin, for the first time gin. When before it was juice and water. Suddenly he cannot wait to be away from her. The air on the veranda is thick with the smell of the girl. Her translucent touch. He cannot think straight. He picks up a glass.

"How do you take it?"

"On the rocks."

He nods. He pours in the gin. The girl is sitting now. He gives her the drink. She takes it from his hand while averting her gaze. He sits down across from her and crosses his legs at the ankles. He is aware that he has failed. The girl will not even look at him. So there it is. Two weeks ago his father asked did he not think the girl pretty. Now she is here in the house and he is half wondering how to make her leave.

He says that he will go to find his father and this time she lets him go. She drops her hand through the air to show him just how little she cares. He can go hang himself for all she cares, that is what she is saying. Concealment not being part of the game at present, whatever game it is they are playing. She adjusts her legs, slyly, silk brushing against silk, and does not watch him as he goes.

He finds his father at the front of the house. He has just returned from examining the pools in the river. He is wearing his work clothes and his shirt is open to expose his barrel-chested girth. Tom tells him that the girl is here. He nods and then asks Tom why he is not with her. Before Tom responds he strides through the hall, his boots leaving long streaks of mud on the floor.

Tom makes a note to himself to tell Jose to clean the marks up. Now, immediately. While they are easy to wipe away. He turns to look for Jose. He walks the house in a hurry, looking for him. He finds him at last, out back, and he whispers the instructions. About the mud. In the hall. Then he returns to the veranda.

The girl stands, back against a pillar, dress lifting on the wind, and she does not turn at the sound of Tom's footsteps. He stops at the door. His father is at the liquor trolley. He pours with a steady hand. He picks the girl's drink up from the table and hands it to her. She takes it with a nod. The old man does not look at her. He stands beside her and takes in her view. He takes of her space. Eventually, she turns to him.

Tom watches, from the doorway. He stares, from the darkness. And then he leaves them. He goes to see that Jose has wiped away the mud and that dinner is prepared for three. When he tells him, Jose does not have the courtesy to look surprised. He says to him the table has already been set.

His father beds the girl every night for the next three weeks. A native brings her two trunks. The Wallaces themselves do not appear. His father has made some arrangement—clearly his father has made some arrangement. It is true the girl has no reputation to lose and it is also true the situation does not necessarily look so bad. She is engaged to Tom. She has a place on the farm while she recovers her health and then there is the difficulty of adjusting to the life in the valley.

Which is different. Different to what she knows and not so different after all. Because she has already found her way. She is a girl who lands on her feet.

Tom walks the house and does his best to avoid her. Naturally he runs into her at every turn. She wanders the halls in

a state of growing undress. A hair ribbon that has come undone, a strap that has fallen loose. It gets worse—much worse,
until she is walking the halls, dragging herself from room to
room, draping herself on the chairs and settees in nothing
more than the excuse of a dressing gown. Sometimes not
even that. Sometimes nothing more than a chemise and Tom
swears it is worse than if she had been naked.

She is like a bitch in heat. The same smell comes off the
animals during mating season. Then they run across the land,
eyes rolling back in their heads, sick and made foul with desire. They have to lock the dogs away when they are like this.
There is nothing else for it. They should do the same to the
girl only it is too late and the fever has already set in. Into all
of them, into the walls of the house.

Soon, within a matter of days, she finds her way into his
mother's wardrobe. Silk dresses and fur wraps and clothes,
clothes far more costly than those she arrived in. Now every
evening she dresses for dinner. She puts on a chiffon frock,
she draws the tasseled belt tight. The colors are rich and the
fabrics delicate and they are cut in the complicated way that
means quality. Tom has an eye for such things. Generally useless but now put into practice.

He scans her every night and soon he notices that there are
jewels, there are diamonds and emeralds, hanging from her
slender wrist and neck, tucked up into her hair. She arrives
with tortoiseshell clips and sapphire rings, she is practically
glittering when she comes down to dinner, a shiny, ghostly
apparition in his mother's clothes. There are clear differences

between the two women. Nonetheless, Tom sees his father's gaze clamp onto her.

Now his father walks her to the table each night. She sits between Tom and his father, Tom at one end of the table, his father at the other, and the girl sitting between them. She will take Tom's place. In no time she will be sitting across from the old man and presiding over the table. With her newfound airs and graces. Already she is playing the lady of the house and is surprisingly good at it.

Every night he walks the halls and there is a nightmare of sounds emanating from his father's bedroom. Sickly moans and thumps in the night. Suckling and animal bellowing. The stuff of nightmares, which he remembers from childhood. He stands outside his father's door. He lowers his head and listens. The noise is loud, the house and all the rooms are full with things, bureaus and sofas and carpets, but the sound travels just like the building is hollow.

He does not know how he will face the girl in the morning and still he does. Every morning she looks smug and suddenly well fed. Stuffed—that is one way of putting it. He understands some things about the situation. That he was marked for the fool from the start. That this was always part of the plan. That they are right to view him with contempt. No doubt they are laughing at him now, from the dampness of their bed.

Father knows best. The scales on Tom's skin erupt for the first time in many years. It is a bad attack. He cannot sleep for the itching. He patrols the house instead, scratching at his hands, he does it for hours and it is only when the sun is rising that he goes to bed. His bedroom is on the opposite side of the house to his father's. There are hundreds of yards between them. But now he goes to bed and the sounds follow him to sleep. He hears it all—the mysterious thumping, the shouts and moans, the loud, loud bellowing.

3

Across the border there is a mountain—and one morning the mountain explodes. First there is an enormous boom. The boom is not hollow but dense with noise. The natives come out of their quarters. They are standing outside, looking and listening, when the boom repeats and then dissolves into a rumble. They are watching when the top of the mountain opens and disgorges fire.

They have never seen this before. Violence from men they understand well, but from the land itself—the mountain now retching, the innards of the earth shooting up—they do not know what to think or how to understand it. A giant cloud of smoke pushes up and covers the sky. Bolts of lightning snap through the cloud. A column of red and orange forms in the middle. The fire pours straight into the sky and fills it.

They feel the explosions that follow from across the border. The ground bucking beneath their feet. They thrust their hands into the air. They try to regain balance. The explosions follow in quick succession and above them the sky is purple and orange and gray and white. They watch. Their hands are shaking and they kneel—are thrust to the ground—in prayer. Even the ones who have no religion to speak of.

The volcano erupts for four days. In the chaos of the four days and darkness the farmers let go of their routine. The live-stock go unfed and then are fed at strange hours of the night. It makes them bellow in fear. They stampede across the lot and then huddle together and then stampede again. Also, they shit constantly. Streams of shit pouring out of their bodies as they squeal and grunt.

The natives are sent out to calm the herds. They press themselves between the animal bodies. They step into soft piles of shit—the shit goes as high as their ankles, it goes as high as their calves. They stroke and soothe and croon but cannot take their eyes from the sky. They wonder if it will last forever. If it will never stop. The animals can sense their dis-traction and are not comforted.

When four days pass the mountain's contractions slow. It takes another two days for the cloud to ease and they see patches of sky for the first time. There is sunlight. The con-tractions slow again and then stop. The animals are calm—the natives and farmers alike take that to be a sign, but they still doubt the sun and sky. Four days and they are numb to the life that came before.

The mountain had been silent for a thousand years. They did not know it could explode. They had been trained to worry about other things. The ravages of colonialism. Man-made apocalypse, nuclear disaster—they have seen pictures, they have heard stories. They are not educated people in the valley and the natives in particular are prone to modern superstition. They worry about their skin and hair and wonder if they will drop dead in ten years' time, a reaction delayed.

They are reading the wrong signs. The right signs have nothing to do with history or culture. Two days before the eruption the snakes fled down the mountain. They slid, then dropped into the river and drowned. Within hours they were washing up on the dirt banks of the river. Stiff and twisted like small branches of wood, their bodies rigid in death.

The news of the snakes moved slowly. The villagers in the neighboring country were too busy gathering the bodies of the snakes, which they collected with their bare hands in baskets and then threw onto the fire like wood. They were too busy and so the volcano came to the valley first, before the news of the snakes that slithered down the mountain. The news of the snakes came with the ash. The ash and the slow clearing sky.

ON THE EIGHTH day the ash arrives in the country. It is quiet for four days. The mountain belching only a pocket or two of black smoke. The ground staying still. But then the ash happens.

It creeps across the border and into the country. It does it in the night, by stealth. The farmers in the valley wake and there is a thick layer of gray on the ground and in the air. They are baffled. It looks like snow but it is still hot outside and the gray is too fine. It is hard to see, almost invisible to the eye. Like a dry fog. Dry to the touch and everywhere in the air. They wave their hands through the air and their skin is parched.

By noon the valley is lost to a blizzard of ash. The children and the local imbeciles put on swimming trunks and goggles and run through the ash. They try to make balls of it. The ash balls fall to pieces in their hands and they throw handfuls of dust instead. They run across the fields and their feet slip and they choke on the dust. In places they fall to their waists in ash. They are laughing like loons, their minds cracked.

The ash continues to fall and the layer grows higher. It does not freeze into solid tranches. It does no melting of any kind. It only accumulates. The roads and tracks close themselves up. The car motors eat up dust and die. The bicycle wheels do not turn. They try to clear paths but the ash keeps falling. It is up to their waists, up to their necks. Two children disappear into the ash and are not found.

After two days, there is a brief respite in the ash fall and the men go out into the landscape. They try to clear paths. They fill wheelbarrows with the ash and cart it away, briefly they try to make order of it. Then the storm picks up and the ash plain grows higher and they retreat inside again. From the houses the windows show nothing but a field of gray without sky or ground. They look out the windows and give up. They bar themselves in their homes and watch the ash horizon climb up the walls of the houses.

One week later the ash slows. The farmers and natives step out into the monochrome landscape. Which was once their home. Which is all they know. They wear scarves and gas masks to protect themselves from the swirl of ash in the air. The particles minute and lingering. Then they embark on the task of rescuing the landscape from the ash. Digging it out like an archeological site: the evidence of their lives.

The real miracle is the fact that so many of the animals survived. The prescient put them in the barns. They left a native to stay with them through the ash storm. Feeding them daily. Avoiding them when they bucked and stomped in panic. Finally the ash stops falling and they release them into the open air. Onto the gray plain. Their legs buckle and their knees give into the dust. But they press forward, they find their footing, and disappear across the field.

THE FIRST DAY the mountain exploded, the old man held drinks at the farm. Among the whites, across the valley, there was a mood of hilarity. The girl said that company was what they needed and word was sent out. Dinner was ordered and the liquor trolley stocked. The neighboring whites—those who remained and were not afraid to travel—came at dusk and Jose served drinks on the veranda.

The men came without their wives, this being no time for a woman to travel. They stood with a drink in their hand and admired the view. On the whole the old man did not fraternize with these small landowners. These whites owned small plots of land and were therefore considered grasping. They had survived in the land through bluntness and cunning and were now starting to come into their own, what with the change taking place in the province.

They were men suited to this new age of violence. They were mobile and unreliable, with a reputation for physical brutality. There were fistfights and beatings on their farms and there had been shootings. The old man said they were men who did not understand the boundaries of behavior. But the girl liked society and they were now what passed for society in the valley. Therefore they had been invited to the farm.

It was almost a gathering like the old days, before the first departures and the unrest, before the rumors of possible rebellion. There was candlelight and crystal. There was in front of them a vast expanse of land. However, the men were tense. They stood on the veranda and watched the mountain tear into the sky. They talked but mostly drank from nervousness. They began with cocktails and then there was wine at dinner. After dinner there were ports and liqueurs.

The girl played jazz records on the gramophone and watched as the nervous men grew drunk. The scene loosened into a facsimile of the life back home. A poor one, the blacks and grays blurring into the white. A certain amount of play acting being involved. That play acting being imprecise. The girl smiled when the men made toasts to the mountain. She smiled again when the old man brought out a box of cigars and the men made toasts to the cigars.

Jose filled their glasses. The night progressed. The men were drunk but still restrained. The girl also. She had no intention of being reckless. She stood up and walked the veranda. She was not wearing very much. Her body exposed by her dress (his mother's dress). Tom watched her and grew an ache in his throat and groin. She saw him watching and went to the old man. She sat down beside him on a stool.

In the morning, the men were still on the veranda. They had passed out in their armchairs. The old man ordered lunch for the party. The men nodded thanks without getting to their feet, and did not think of leaving the farm. Then it was noon and the sky was still dark and lit with fire. Lightning cracked up through the sky. They could see rivers of lava and the black cap of smoke continued to grow up above.

The men sat in the old man's house and watched the mountain explode. Jose moved down the line of armchairs. He pushed a cart of drinks and then brought trays of cold food. The men ate and drank. The air now bearing permissiveness of a new kind. The men visibly inhaling it. It was hot, and they untucked and unbuttoned their shirts. There was not much conversation. One of the men said they might bring their wives for dinner, the roads seeming safe enough. He used the telephone to ring back to his farm and word was sent round.

There were eight men on the veranda that day and all eight stayed into the night. At dusk their wives were driven to the farm by their natives. They had dressed for the special occasion. With satin dresses and wraps to protect against the night air. A table was set in the dining room and dinner was served. Now that the women had come the atmosphere of nervous privilege was restored. The men made toasts to that privilege and proceeded to drink themselves blind.

After dinner the gramophone was switched on again and there was dancing and more drink. The girl came down after dinner. She had stayed in her room all day—trays were sent at mealtimes and endless pots of tea—but now she emerged. She was wearing a new dress, she had arranged her hair so that it looked like it was falling but was not. There was rouge on her cheeks and lips and she had put kohl on her eyes and smelled strongly of scent.

She was not even the most beautiful woman on the veranda. But she wove through the crowd and she had been emboldened by the previous night and there are things besides beauty. For example, the drunken lust of men. Which filled the veranda. Having been so good, the girl was now restless. The presence of the other women had spurred her instinct for competition. Therefore she moved across the veranda and she made the other women disappear. Nothing doing with their lace and ribbon and powder.

Abruptly, the old man stood up. He announced he was retiring for the night. He had no intimation of what was to come, such a thing being impossible for his arrogance to fathom. The other men nodded and watched him disappear across the veranda. The sour stench rising from their armpits. They had done no more than stand in the washroom and sponge their faces and necks. Their clothes still smelled of alcohol and animal must. They were forgetting where they were and making themselves at home.

Always a bad sign. The gramophone cranked. The girl danced down the length of the veranda. The men watched with drunken intent and the women watched, too. The girl did not notice about the men but did about the women. She laughed. Never having had a husband, she had therefore never worried about losing one. She was a little drunk. One of the women abruptly rose to her feet and crossed the veranda.

The other women followed. They were not going to sit and watch their husbands with the girl. The husbands' thoughts being legible to the wives. The wives knowing what the husbands were capable of, having had a lifetime to learn. The women were outraged but the outrage was a cover—there were things happening that they had no interest in seeing. As they left they were aware of having stayed too long as was.

The men were left alone with the girl and she gave a special shimmy to celebrate her victory. Laughter rang out across the veranda. The girl turned up the volume on the gramophone and said something about cigars. One of the men found the box and lighter. The girl passed the box around and the men lit their cigars. Which smoldered and smoked as they watched her. She had stopped dancing and stood smiling as she rubbed her wrists against the jut of her hip.

The record on the gramophone clicked off. The men smoked their cigars in silence and looked at the girl. When they had met her the day before she had stood between the old man and his son and blushed for the duration of the introduction. They hadn't known what to think. The girl seemed simple enough but what was happening between the two men was nothing simple. Not a rivalry as such. For a time they could not understand it.

But now that confusion lifted and they saw the girl for what she was: a spreader of unrest and confusion. The girl was a woman. She was a body—just a body, and evidently a gifted one. All the parts being in working order. The shoulder and neck, the legs and waist and back. (The girl also enjoyed her body. She had faith in it. It was hard as a rock and impenetrable, and thus far it had served her well.)

The girl stood before the men. One stood and came to her and she smiled as he approached. He laid a hand on her shoulder. Gently, he pushed one strap down and then the other. In a manner that was almost inconsequential. He chucked her under the chin and looked into her face. The girl was still smiling as he stepped back and looked at his handiwork and then the girl stopped.

Doubt crossed her face, if anyone had been there to notice. But there was no one—the room was empty in that respect. So the doubt stayed on her face. Doubt as to what was presently unfolding. It was on her face when she kicked off one shoe and then the other shoe (they were pinching, they were hurting so, she did not think she could stay in them one second longer). It was on her face as the shoes skittered across the floor and came to a stop.

The men stared at the shoes. They were tiny. Tiny things of leather and satin. There was a logic to the shoes. Quality and all that. Standards. Propriety. Everything that was currently escaping them—the very idea of being civilized itself—as they sat in their armchairs and watched the girl. They stared at the shoes and then they raised their eyes and looked at the girl.

WHO WAS NOT having an easy time of it and therefore kept her head high and her back rigid. She was conscious of the cool tile beneath her bare feet. The gust of wind through her armpits. The dress was now hanging off her nipples, her nipples were now all that stood between decency and nakedness and lucky for her they were spectacularly erect. Her nipples were a matter of note. Always had been.

She laughed. It sounded hysterical in the silence and she stopped, mouth dry. Truth be told her sense of humor had deserted her. There was plenty to laugh about but she wasn't laughing. She could see the humor, she could see the jokes and punch lines. A woman standing in front of a man, that was already good for some laughs. But she was not in the mood for laughter. She shivered, even though it was hot.

One month ago she arrived in the country and she saw there was nothing here she could not handle, nothing beyond the arid air. She had been warned that it was wild country going wilder, but she had already survived the drawing rooms at home. Home being a ruthless territory, cruelty on display with the silk and china. She had almost been relieved by the barren expanse of country. She had not thought—did not think—that men could be changed by means of landscape.

But now here she was and for the first time she sensed that this was something different, of which she did not have the measure. Something she did not currently understand. Later she would look back on this moment and she would see that there were a hundred things she might have done, at this moment as with any moment, at this moment which was just like any other moment. But then her mind was blank. Small and hard and blank. Like a pebble. Her mind was a pebble. Nothing adhered to its surface.

So she did what she always did. When her mind was blank, when the sickness set in, when her skin began to itch and burn. What she always did, a woman's only purchase on power. She took her clothes off. She reached up her hands and undid the hook and eye closure. She pulled down the zipper of her dress, this cunningly designed dress, more expensive than anything she had ever owned.

It was going to happen anyway so she might as well be the one to do it. Not that she was a fatalist but the zipper slid down without protest and now the dress was hanging off her back. Taking off your clothes was easy. Putting them back on was the hard part. Now look. She was down to her skivvies and they were not clean. It didn't matter. She could sing a song and nobody would notice. Children should be seen and not heard. The saying referred strictly to the girls, the girls who would grow up to be ladies.

Not that she was a lady. She was, however, a product of her society. It was getting hard to think, hard to figure it out, because now there was wetness growing. A slick between her legs and the thrall of physical longing. Well, a woman felt the weight of a man looking, a woman liked to be wanted, and here were several men, here a group of men. Who could see the wetness for all she knew.

She exhaled and tried to keep her head straight. Lust and the mistakes that were made in its wake. A trail of them, each bigger than the last. Desire was what plagued women, it was what tripped them up. She thought: a woman should seek out dry land. Be rid of lust at last. Which made nothing good or clear. Which only gathered around a woman, inutile and collecting dust. Men did not like the women who wanted it. Men would rather force themselves on the women who didn't. The logic being dismal but clear.

At the same time, a man would take what he could get and always did. One of the men stood up. She raised her head to look at him. He was plain, he was nothing as a man. He moved slowly, with both hands spread before him. Like he thought she was a rabbit or a rabid animal. She watched and saw the gleam flicker into his eyes. Her body relaxed a notch. After all they were men. After all they were the same. She smiled and then she watched his face harden in front of her and the smile died on her lips.

She stood in the blast of hunger that came from his body and the hatred coming from his eyes. Hatred for her as a woman. She became afraid. Panic swung through her body and then she changed her mind. A woman can change her mind, she thought. A woman can get wet between the legs and loosen her dress and she still has the right to change her mind. Doesn't she? Isn't that what they said?

She felt the situation slipping out of her control. She stumbled and tried to guess at the damage. There was the old man. They were afraid of him—that could work for her or against her, likely against. She had seen the store of resentment in the faces of the men. Built over time and carefully fortified. Brick by brick and then the wall broke and wiped out whatever stood in its way. Due to either bad luck or stupidity.

She had made a situation for herself on the farm and a good one. But now it was turning to mud and faster than she could believe. It was not fate and not inevitable but it was what was going to happen. Now the man was standing in front of her. He walked his eyes across her body and then to her face. The interest being more knot than attraction. His lust being caught up in complicated things. Like power and shame and fear. She thought: we are not so different. I know you, there are things that we share.

She wasn't even convincing herself. His gaze slid around her neck to her back and his body followed, his body circled round. He stood behind her. She closed her eyes as he gripped her neck. With the other hand he yanked her to him. Held her by the neck and pushed her dress aside. Rooted downstairs. Poked a finger in. Slapped it with an open hand. Hard, not teasing like, not affectionate. She gasped and winced in pain. She thought: surely not here, in front of all of them. Surely not like this.

He unbuckled his trousers and shoved right into her but she was wet so it wasn't rape. Which gave him no pleasure or less pleasure or a different pleasure to the one he was wanting. So that was a point for the girl. Just one but who was counting, you grasped at straws when you were trying to keep your head on your shoulders. Now he was calling her a whore cunt bitch but she'd heard it all before. Nothing new under the sun, nothing he could tell or show her. With his idiot thrusting.

Like a dog or rat or pig. Quick as a dog, too, and it was on to the next one.

So that was how it was going to be. So she was going to be sore but she had her pills. A whole bottle of them on the bed stand in her room. One of the men slapped her face and pushed her to the ground. She concentrated on the pills. She should have counted how many. How many pills and how many men. In case there was an equivalence lurking in the numbers. Back when this began, which already felt like a long time ago.

Were they all going to take their turn? Was every one of them going to line up for a poke and a stab? Or had some of the group left—scared by what they wanted to see and what they would imagine for weeks to come, what they almost saw and did. She tried to keep count. It took her mind off things, which were quickly becoming painful back there. Desire ran out on you and then the fucking started. You could disconnect but there was nothing like pain to bring you back.

Not that she wanted them to stop. She couldn't think a thought so clearly. She couldn't think her way past the situation at hand, she could no longer fathom what happened next.

To give her credit: she was not waiting to be saved. She was not waiting for the shout of a man coming to save her from another man. (Which would have had nothing to do with her. A man saved a woman and he was only saving some idea of himself. A man was nothing but a continent of ideas. Whereas a woman lived on shifting ground. Therefore it was easy to slip between the cracks. They'd been warning her since she was a child. She couldn't say she hadn't been told.)

There was no sound of feet. No slam of door. No anger. No stopping. It went on. What a body can take is always more than a body can take until it isn't. Until the body says it can do no more. Her body went past that point and she knew nothing about it. Her head had disconnected from her body and was floating in space. Her arms and legs were next and then it was just her torso—she'd forgotten her torso, she had left it behind. With the wolf pack snapping at her heels. Snapping and then biting and then eating and she was gone.

Outside, the mountain was decapitated by flame. The smoke cloud blotted out the sky. None of the men on the veranda looked at the mountain. They were otherwise occupied.

4

In the morning five men left and three stayed behind. The five who left woke early. They dressed by low light and went downstairs, whispering and motioning in silence. Tiptoeing in their socks. They found the old man sitting at a table on the veranda eating breakfast. In the background the volcano was still electric orange and the sky was still black.

They came to the table with their boots in their hands and told the old man they were going. They had their own farms to attend to. The old man nodded. They thanked him for his hospitality. He offered them breakfast. It was a visible after-thought. The men said no. The old man nodded and turned back to his paper. News came to the valley late, the papers a week old by the time they reached the farm.

The five men pulled on their boots and were silent as they went down the veranda steps. Once they got to the track their gait relaxed. When they got a little further one of them started to whistle. A tune from last night's gramophone. A little snippet of song. The others joined in. They formed a five-part harmony and galloped down the road.

Five men left and three stayed behind. Like Job's comforters. They appeared at noon, each grasping a sheet of newspaper. They stood on the veranda and surrounded the old man. Who sat rooted in his chair. He did not consider himself to be trapped, he showed no evidence of that belief. But he remained surrounded by the men all day, unable to shake them off and wearing an expression of deepening outrage.

Tom did not understand what was going on. Tom had not been on the veranda the previous night. He had been on the other side of the house. Confined to his bedroom with a severe case of indigestion. He spent the evening lying on the bed in a sweat. Every ten minutes he lurched to the toilet and emptied his bowels. Temporarily relieved, he dragged himself back to the bed, only to lurch up again shortly after.

This kind of thing was always happening to Tom. The result was always the same: Tom was the only one who did not know. He woke in the morning and noticed that something was wrong. Half the men had gone and the men who stayed were different. They had changed overnight. They were emboldened and they patrolled the house like they had the owning of it. They were no longer shamed by the old man, by the house and the farm, but Tom did not understand why.

He did not see the girl all day but that was not unusual. She slept until evening and did not like to be disturbed. Tom had often thought: a man could murder her in the night and the body would not be found until next evening. A man could creep into her room and take a cleaver to her head. Be away by morning, in a new country by noon. It could be done. There had been rumors of such things. They would spend days looking for a bloodstained native.

Tom had a bad sense of humor. Another one of his flaws. However, the humor was intermittent, a nervous habit that soon gave way to anxiety. Two days passed and still the girl did not appear. He asked Celeste about it. She said the girl was indisposed and then shook her head. Tom asked if they should call for a doctor and she shook her head again. Ah no, she said. No doctors. No doctors, he repeated. No doctors.

Tom looked for his father. He found him on the veranda with the three men. The sight of the old man surrounded unnerved Tom. He thought: the presence of the men and the absence of the girl. He did not go out onto the veranda but he stood and saw. His father's face red with anger as he read the newspaper again and again. One of the men leaned forward, his hand on the old man's shoulder. Tom strained to hear his words.

"You see it right there."

The old man did not respond.

"You see the steps that are being taken."

"I see nothing."

The man leaned back and crossed his arms.

"The Government will concede."

The old man looked up angrily.

"On what authority? To whose demands?"

The man remained calm. He smiled and pried the

newspaper from the old man's hands. The old man's face darkened at the audacity. The man ignored him. He folded the paper in two and tucked it into his pocket for safekeeping. Then he looked down at the old man.

"Try to imagine it. If we do not make concessions, they will tear this country to pieces."

Tom shook his head and stepped away. It was no time to be worrying about the news. Going over the matter of the unrest yet again. Four days after the mountain began to erupt and two days after the girl took ill, the volcano stopped. Across the valley there was relief. But on the farm the situation remained unchanged. The men showed no signs of departing. And the old man strangely powerless against them.

It was like the farm had seized up with cramp. It needed to be moved back into life. Grasped by the middle and jolted. It was not something Tom could do, it needed the old man's force. There never having been anything like this before. As it was, Tom was already unnerved. He did not like having strangers in the house. He was constantly moving from room to room in order to avoid them. While the old man remained fixed to the veranda, examining the week-old newspaper.

Tom went to Jose and told him they would ride to the High Point. From there they would be able to see the mountain and assess how the land had been damaged. The old man prided himself on his knowledge of the land. His best self was a man patrolling his land astride a horse. He was therefore bound to join them. In this way Tom would recover his father. He would detach him from the rubber grip of the three men.

However, Tom's plan failed. He went to the old man's study early the next morning and found the old man already surrounded by his comforters. Tom had never seen a stranger in his father's rooms. Now there were three. Three, standing in the room. Sitting on the desk. Looking out the window. Tom stopped at the door and could go no further. His father looked up.

"What is it?"

"We are going to the High Point."

His father nodded. He didn't move.

"When?"

"Now. Or when you like."

A pause. His father looked down at the sheets of paper on the desk. He shuffled them vaguely. Tom kicked at the door-jamb for his attention.

"Will you join us?"

His father shook his head. He did not look up—he waved Tom away with his eyes still on the papers. Tom backed out of the room. He turned and heard the air whistling through his ears. He almost stumbled in the hall but righted himself. He went to meet Jose at the stables. They led their rides out in silence. It was only when they had mounted the horses that Jose turned to him.

"Where is he?"

"He's not coming."

Jose nodded. He did not look surprised and did not say anything further. Although they had been brought up together, of the same age and both nursed at Celeste's tit, Jose was a mystery to Tom. Fatherless Jose, halfway an orphan, who nonetheless understood things Tom could not comprehend. When Tom looked at Jose he saw nothing but an opaque surface: the obstruction of things Jose knew, that Tom could not hope to know. In silence, they turned the horses out and headed to the High Point.

In the wake of the volcano, the landscape was muted but not quiet. There were sounds throughout and the sky had the density of the ocean. Tom thought: there was water everywhere, and waves up in the sky. Around them the farm was calm. As they climbed they could see the force of the old man's imprint on the terrain: the fences corralling the fields, the plow marks in the dirt. The sky churned overhead but down on the surface things were almost as before. The horses shied when a hawk swooped down across the path. The two men calmed the horses and pressed forward up the valley.

They reached the High Point ten minutes later. There, the landscape reared up violently. The ground a lunging beast but worse. The mountain looming in front of them, the top blown off and rivulets of lava still flowing. Tom looked across at it. He realized that things had changed. The ground had come undone and lacked all coherence, it rolled forward in senseless disorder. They had seen none of it from the valley. They'd had no idea of its scale.

It was like they had crossed into another world. Tom in particular was not prepared. He did not have the tools to understand what he now saw. He had never been anywhere in his life. Barely having left the farm, a city street would have struck him like a miracle.

"What will happen now?"

He barely spoke the words, he wasn't sure he said them at all. Jose shook his head.

"No person knows."

"What does that mean?"

"There has never been anything like this."

Tom looked down at the river. He could see that it was black and brown with debris. Close to the mountain it hardly seemed to run at all. As if it had turned to mud. As if it would turn to stone. The mud river, the stone river, ran down from the mountain and toward the border. Over the border and into their land. Quickly, Tom looked at Jose.

"There is something wrong with the river."

Jose took a long time in responding. Then Tom realized he was not going to respond at all. He was not looking at the river but up at the sky. He was staring at its churning brightness like he was waiting to go blind.

"What is it?"

He shook his head.

"What is it?"

Tom spoke more forcefully this time. Jose stared at the ground and still did not respond. Then he shook his head.

"Nothing good."

"Nothing good? That's all you have to say?"

Jose nodded.

"Nothing good."

"About the river? Are you talking about the river? There is something wrong with it."

"Nothing good about nothing."

Tom kicked the horse and it bolted down the path. After a second, he heard Jose follow. Tom laughed. To have asked so many times. To have made himself ridiculous. What had made him think the man knew something, something about the mountain and the farm, something Tom could not see? If the natives had instinct, they had cunning, and the two added up to nothing.

His father never had these difficulties. He gave orders and the natives listened because they knew the old man had no want he could not satisfy himself. Tom was different. He could do nothing of his own. He needed the servants and they were aware of this, having had many years to realize the fact. Tom was their superior but on the farm they were all subordinate to the old man. However. Tom reminded himself that would change, that would all be changing, soon. His father had promised him as much.

He was calmed by the thought. They took the horses down the slope and to the stables. The horses were skittish. They tossed their heads and once Tom was almost unseated. When they returned to the house they saw the men on the veranda. His father looked up when Tom approached. He said that they should order dinner for five. Beef, as there was no fish. He supposed there was still the foie gras and the caviar. He said to bring out whatever was left.

That night, the ash began. It happened in the middle of

the night. Tom was asleep. He woke to the sound of footfall. People banging doors in the night. He pulled on his trousers and stepped into the hall. The servants were running, shouting to each other. He pulled on his shirt and hurried after them. Out in the main rooms of the house it was chaos. Everyone was awake. He spun around and grabbed the nearest person.

"What is it? What has happened?"

He was speaking to some boy—the foreman's son, he thought. The boy shook his head. He pointed outside. Over the veranda. The air outside was white with ash. He dropped the boy's arm at the sight of it. He did not understand. It fell thick as snow but he knew immediately that this was no snowfall. He had never seen such fine stuff airborne. It fell like rain then swirled like snow. The rapid shifts incomprehensible to him.

He looked down at his feet. He watched the ash scurry into the house. A fine coating on the lawn. A little heap on the steps. The ash was ten feet away. As he watched it came closer, covering inches and then feet within a matter of seconds. He stood still and watched as the dust swept to his toes and then over his feet like he was sculpture in a garden.

He swung his head up to look outside: the air was stiller than before. It had grown thicker. More opaque. The lights from the house lit the dust several yards deep. Then the world dropped into darkness. He could see nothing of it. No shadow or contour—it was not normal, it was not natural, this dark.

He was now coated in dust to his calves. It unfolded like a scene from the horror movies he watched as a child. They gave him deep and penetrating nightmares—his father used to laugh at the way the terror made him cower from sleep. The way it made him wet his bed in the night. Tom looked past the veranda in the direction of the river. He grabbed another passing boy by the arm.

"Where is my father? Is he awake?"

The boy stared at him. He shook him hard.

"Go and wake him. Go and get him."

The boy didn't move.

"Go!"

The boy turned and scurried away. The boy had not left the room before the old man emerged in boots and a dressing gown, his hair disheveled. He didn't look at Tom. He barreled forward across the hall. He crossed the veranda, jumped down the steps and into the airborne sea of ash. He disappeared in an instant and was gone. Tom peered through the mist. His father had been swallowed by the swell of ash. There was no trace of him at all.

Beside him, two servants were shouting to each other. They spoke too quickly for him to hear.

"What is it?"

They turned to him.

"The dust—he will not be able to breathe. It will get into his eyes. His lungs."

He stared at them for a moment. Then he lunged forward across the veranda and into the dust. Some of the men followed him. The last thing he heard was their feet moving on the stone floor behind him. Then he was enveloped by the dust. In an instant he heard and saw nothing. He was only floating through space. It was quiet, he had dreamed of it as a child, sometimes it came to him still—the dream of being untethered.

An instant later his mouth was full of dust and he was choking, coughing, splattering up tears and phlegm. He stumbled over the ash—there were mounds of it across the ground, several inches in places, gathering with speed. He flung his arms out. Like he was looking for a wall to lean against. He felt the men enter the cloud of dust behind him—insulated explosions, the sign of distant movement. The silence remained unbroken.

His eyes—now open to slivers—adjusted and he saw things. Gradations of color. Pools of light. He stumbled forward, arms spread wide. He called for his father. Ash flew into his mouth and he coughed again. He heard nothing. There was only a dense and regular throbbing. The ash already too much. He squeezed his eyes and mouth shut, he pressed his palms into his face, trying to cough out the dust.

Tears streamed down his face. He was finding it hard to breathe, he saw for the first time that he might suffocate. He told himself he knew the land well. Each inch of soil and every rock beyond was familiar to him. He pressed forward. He knew his father had gone to the river. There was nowhere else he could have gone. He had seen it in the old man's face— once he had seen the ash in the air and on the ground.

The other men carried electric torches and now the light bounced through the darkness. He saw one of them in the mist. A man standing in a pool of light. It was Jose. He was bare-chested and had wrapped his shirt around his head. He stopped and motioned to Tom. He waved his hand through the air, around his head. His hand, coated in dust. Tom stripped off his shirt and wrapped it, mimicking Jose, around his mouth and eyes. He breathed easier, into the cotton fabric of his shirt.

He left one eye uncovered and using this one eye he continued in the direction of the river. The landscape had grown alien. He had never seen any of what he saw now. The ground he had always known—this place, the only thing he had ever seen or understood—had vanished. He accepted that he knew nothing of where he was. He thought this was what blindness must be like. Nothing complete or total. The field, constantly shifting, and small gradations of light and shadow.

Then he saw a fragment of the old man. An arm that appeared and then disappeared. A smear of movement that was his back. He saw, in fragments, through the dust: the old man in trouble. He lurched forward toward the shape. Guided by his single eye, his single eye straining to hold the fragments in place. To keep the movement in sight. He started running, knees buckling, arms flailing.

His father dropped out of his field of vision. He stopped and looked around him. He yanked the shirt from his face and shouted.

"Father!"

The dust flew into his face. Into his eyes and he was blinded. He coughed violently. The men moved in his direction at the

sound. He felt the vibration of their movement. He continued shouting for his father. The dust flew into his mouth and
muffled the sound of his cries.

"Father!"

He swung his body round. Shouting in all directions. The
men were close, he could feel them coming closer. He opened
his mouth and screamed again, through the ash.

"Father!"

He tripped over the body. There it was the whole time,
all this time—closer than he'd thought or realized. He knelt
down and found an arm, a torso. He could not see so he went
by touch. The cord of neck, the wings of his chest. The body
jumped and rasped. Tom leaned closer. He could not remember the last time he had touched his father's body. He gripped
it through the ash.

He began brushing the ash away with one hand and then
with both. He swept off handfuls of ash to reveal a patch
of collar. A piece of skin. An open mouth. He brushed and
brushed and uncovered his father piece by piece. He claimed a
shoulder, a chin. Then a new sweep of ash covered him again.

Still he kept brushing at him, like a dog uncovering a bone.
The ash was gathering in Tom's throat. He coughed. The old
man's eyes were watering and they were turning the ash to
mud on his skin. His mouth a smear of damp dust. Tom sat
back. He gave up and watched as the ash covered his father. He
watched it coating his face until it disappeared. In the distance,
he heard the men moving in his direction.

"Here! Here!"

He tried to lift him up. He hoisted him up in his arms. The body bucked with a cough and slid out of his arms. He flopped back to the ground. Tom lifted him again, arms twisting as the old man writhed and slipped downward again. Tom had never realized how heavy his father was. His weight was supernatural. Like he was made from lead and malicious in unconsciousness.

Tom's own body collapsed under its weight. He called out to the men again.

"Here! He is here!"

They arrived from all sides, like an ambush: men emerging from the swirl of ash. They surrounded the father and son. They were grainy silhouettes, dark shapes against the white cloud and dim light. They carried the electric torches pointing downward and they looked like billy clubs at their thighs. Their heads wrapped in shirts and scarves. Tom thought he saw Jose standing at the back of the group. He called out to him.

The call died in his throat. He saw Jose lift his hand as if to stay the men. They stood in a circle and did not move. Fear seized across Tom's throat. They would die here—it was the most obvious idea in the world. The natives turning on them at last. They would be left to perish in the ash storm. They would suffocate on their own land. A stupid death looking more and more likely as the men gathered and did nothing.

The idea of their resentment never occurred to the old man. Even though there had been incidents—servants killing their own masters in the night, nannies slaughtering their wards—of which the old man was aware. His father's power was too absolute for imagination. Tom, on the other hand, could imagine their resentment with ease. He was aware of how little the natives liked him. In an instant he was flooded with fear. It warped his sense of things and in particular time. It made a second or two seem much longer and it made him hysterical without cause.

He wondered if it would give the men pleasure to watch the two of them die. He thought it would. He couldn't see how it wouldn't. That was the last thought that crossed his mind. Then his throat closed and his consciousness gagged with the strain. He was seized, a cloth pulled across his face to protect his eyes and mouth and nose, all of which were burning. Through the cloth he could hear shouts and see the whirl of ash moving fast past him.

They carried Tom and his father back to the veranda. They dropped them on the floor, in separate piles of ash—it was everywhere, in giant drifts and piles, all across the room—and then set to work pulling the storm doors closed. They moved very quickly. Eyes shut, Tom's fear dissolved and he was once more comforted by the presence of the men. He did not see the look that passed between them. He recovered his breath, lying still in the bed of ash.

The men pulled the storm doors into place and the house was plunged into darkness. The whisper of ash outside. In places the bobbing of the electric torches, the flicker of flame as the lamps and candles were lit. Tom wiped the ash from his face and sat up.

He saw Jose, kneeling beside the old man. He cradled the old man's body in his arms and carefully cleared the ash from his face. The other men ran their hands down his limbs, checking for breaks and cuts. The women were not far behind, they came with cloths and bowls of water and they began wiping the man clean. They were preserving something without even knowing it, not understanding the consequences, as they worked over the old man and brought him back to consciousness.

Tom thought: the old man will live forever because they will it. Only because of that. He felt a throb of jealousy. To be cared for in this way. To be touched. In between the candlelight they moved. One of the women came to Tom and gently pushed him back to the ground. He lay in the bed of ash. She dipped a cloth in water and wrung it out slowly.

The sound of water dripping. She said to him the generator has been clogged by the ash. It is no longer working. But the old man is fine. The old man was safe. Tom nodded. She wiped the cloth across his face and said nothing further. She wiped around his mouth, his forehead. Down his arms and the flakes of horned skin. She cleared the grit from his eyes. He saw Jose, giving orders, organizing the men. He closed his eyes. He lay back. He waited, for now.

5

Two weeks later, his father leaves the farm, taking Jose and the girl with him.

Jose is loading a wagon full of trunks. The girl sits in the wagon bed, wrapped in a shawl. She is propped up on pillows and there is a carafe of tea by her side and an open tin of lobster. She stares straight ahead, eyes blank and cloudy. Her fingers work the fabric of her dress and she trembles very slightly. The weather has changed in the weeks since the volcano exploded.

Jose loads the wagon and his father watches. The old man is wearing a three-piece suit for traveling. A watch and chain and his wallet heavy in his pocket. He is bare headed. He looks and then goes to the girl. He pulls a blanket across her lap and tells her to eat the lobster. She nods and reaches for the tin. Fumbles with a fork and then eats it with her fingers.

His father smokes a cigarette. Jose throws rope across the heap of trunks and valises. He pulls the rope tight and the wagon rocks and creaks. They pile more trunks in. The girl's things. She has been changed but there is still the matter of her trinkets and her objects, pilfered from his mother's wardrobe. They drag behind her, she is barely aware of how they drag behind her. While his father is in the habit of traveling light. Never more than a single suitcase and now look at him.

Two weeks. Two weeks and he has decided to leave. He has split himself from the land, a cleaving formerly thought impossible, a separation still difficult to imagine. But now the wagon creaks with the load it carries, there is a wagon heavy with possessions, the old man is leaving like the other whites—and Tom is staying behind.

IN THE PAST two weeks Tom's fear had grown as the valley recovered and the old man's face grew quiet and watchful. The ash was cleared from the pastures and shoveled from the roofs of the houses. The natives hauled it away in wheelbarrows and made giant heaps on the edge of each village. Then the sky was clear and only the ash heaps stood like obscure markers to the storm.

But on the farm: a record of ongoing catastrophe. When the fish began to float in the river, Tom saw the inverse to everything: the fishing, the food on the table, the money. Everything that had drawn the girl to them in the first place. The dreamlike arms and legs of the river farm, which sat useless in the water, corralling fish that were going nowhere. As the bodies gathered they added pressure and weight until the legs creaked and cracked and then broke.

As soon as the ash stopped the old man sent the natives into the river to retrieve it. They listened to him give the order and stared into the water. They didn't move. They stared at the mass of rotting flesh and turbid sludge. Then they looked at him as if to say: if that was what he ordered (it was). If that was what he wished (it was). They stripped down to the waist and stood on the banks of the river. They waited to see if he would change his mind. He didn't and they tied cloths around their faces and dropped into the water.

They began moving at once. Standing waist deep in the river, they used their hands to push the bobbing fish away. They moved in the direction of the river farm and then fanned out to circle the apparatus. Their faces impassive behind the cloths. Slowly they surrounded the apparatus and then reached for the legs, which were slippery with muck and rot. They turned to pull it toward land.

The apparatus did not move. The fish were too deep in the water. The men were pushing their own legs through the layers of dead fish. They were squeezing through the wall of bodies. Moving in its crevices. They pulled again. The apparatus remained immobile. Their grip slipped on the legs and the machine sank down into the water.

They called to the men watching on the riverbank. They stripped down and plunged into the water. They shouted for rope, which they tied around the legs of the machine. They sent the lightest man to do it. He lay sprawled across the machine, moving from leg to leg, tying knots around each joint. Then he gave a shout and dropped back into the water.

He shouted again and they threw the lengths of rope to the men still standing on land.

They pulled. Slowly the machine rose out of the water. With a grim expression, the men in the river dunked down below the machine and hoisted it above the river of fish. As they rose out of the water they were covered in grime to their faces. Decaying plant and flesh draped from their neck and arms. They shimmied through the dead fish, holding the apparatus above their heads, carrying and pulling it to shore. Then they dropped the machine onto dry soil and stood, reeking of rot and panting from their labor.

The river farm was in ruin. The men were too pleased with their labor to notice at first. They laughed as they wiped the river gunk from their bodies. Chunks of decomposing flesh. All the dying, all around them, became like comedy. They laughed and laughed from relief. They were almost giddy, they were content, as the rot fell from their bodies to the ground.

Into their laughter—his father's cry, a terrible noise. He stood, staring at the machine. Slowly, the men turned and looked. It lay in a heap, groaning. Sputtering. Moaning in death throes. In actual terms the machine was silent but there was sound in the sight of the machine, sprawled out on the ground, legs collapsed, like a street thug had taken a club to each one of its joints.

Tom was also there. And he thought: it had been such a beautiful thing, the first time they had taken it out. They had carried it to the river and set it drifting. The legs had spread

into the water like a living thing and it sat on the river aloft—
the most astonishing thing they had ever seen. A miracle of
technology and time. A piece of the future that had been
shipped to their remote corner of the world. He had seen
the farm's beauty, even if he didn't understand its role in the
farm's future, even if he also feared and hated its purpose.

Now the machine lay in ruin and it took the old man
with it. They saw it happening, it took place right in front of
them. They saw but it was still hard to believe. They looked
at the machine. They looked at the man. They did not believe in his going. The sound, the sound of a man going—it
was everywhere around them. But his face was stoic and his
body straight. He looked stern and unforgiving yet. Then he
turned and walked back into the house, leaving the men and
the machine behind him.

BY THE WAGON, the old man puffs on the cigarette. He watches
Jose continue preparations. Tom feels a churn of rage inside.
From the outside, nothing is visible. But inside he is a jumble
of half words and half deeds. He thinks: I have been running
the farm in all but name. Leave and nothing here will change.
You will see. The land will survive. Also the farm. The natives
will stay here with me. And I will be fine, yes, I will be fine. He
does not believe the words, which enter his head freighted in
confusion.

The girl sits on the pillows and eats from the tin of lobster.
Chunks of shellfish between her thumb and forefinger. She

puts the tin down and wipes her fingers on the blanket. There it is: a real piece of baggage. Living and breathing as it is. Weighing the old man down as it is. Tom bristles just looking at her. She sits among the boxes and the bags and for the first time—through the cloud of rage and panic—Tom sees what his father is taking with him.

A multitude, an ocean of things. The girl is sitting on loot, on things taken—she rides high on the surf of things taken. The loaded wagon material proof of the old man's departure. Tom cannot understand how it has come to this. Two weeks and a lifetime has been undone. He watches his father. The old man circles the wagon. He tests the ropes. The loading is almost done. He takes out his silver watch and checks the dial.

The old man is the same by most known measures. Remote, imperious, unknowable: the same as before. And yet the old man is entirely changed. Despite the disorder in his head, Tom understands something new about his father: that he is a man made visible by means of a backdrop. His father is a shape cut out against a landscape he has personally dominated and formed.

The shape is still the same. It is the backdrop that has gone, and with it everything that makes the man himself. Tom can hardly recognize his father. He cannot see him in the same way, especially now, now that he is leaving, now that he is already parted, has parted himself, from the land and property. It cannot only be Tom. Others must see him differently. A man in bad fortune. His dreams for the future looking foolish. A man without money, which is also ridiculous.

Tom does not know if his father is aware of how he looks. He does not think he cares. His father has been preoccupied. He has stayed to his study. Looking at papers, laying out maps, writing down figures. The old man making midnight telephone calls, the conversations muffled by the house's thick walls so that Tom did not hear the matters being discussed. Although he eavesdropped carefully, diligently.

There was more: the departure of the three men, the day the ash stopped falling. Who left with promises of their return and the strong smell of brilliantine. That afternoon the girl crawled out from her room. She did not look like herself. She was pale and even thinner but the difference was in her eyes. Which had fallen back into her head. She was watching things from a distance, measurably greater than before.

There were other differences. The girl now stayed close to the old man. She was with him all the time. She sat inches away from him at dinner, fork clanging at his plate, fingers reaching for his elbow. The girl standing between the father and the son. Like she was the physical manifestation of the barrier Tom had often tried to deny, but that had always existed between them. As if she were now the guardian of that distance. Tom saw her sitting by the old man's side. He saw her lift up her face to look at him.

They might have shared blood. The girl the old man's daughter. The girl the old man's son, as he might have been, the girl the old man himself. They would stay together. One and one being two. One and one and one on the other hand—it did not add up. Tom did not fit in. In the house there was sunlight and dust so thick it made patterns in the air. He passed the old man's study, he saw the girl and the old man sitting side by side. Neither looked up.

Later, he came upon the girl alone. He stopped and she stopped, too. He looked down at her hand, it was hard for him to look her in the face. She was still wearing his mother's engagement ring. He shook his head in confusion and looked up. Now at her face, which had been wiped blank. She knitted her brow as she looked at him.

"What has happened?"

He intended to sound firm. As if he had some purchase on the situation. He was aware of how close she stood. The fetid smell of her hair.

She shook her head. She had never liked Tom. And they had wanted her to marry him. They had believed this was the solution. Her eyes widened. Briefly. An instant later they receded and she recovered her distance.

Her eyes were once again blank. Not that Tom knew or understood. No details—the details sickened him. He knew that something had happened, that there had been an incident. In this backdrop of new catastrophe. He saw how the girl was and that was enough. He looked at her again.

"Please."

She shook her head. She sighed: the sound like her lungs had broken.

"Do you know—"

She stopped. The girl meant nothing to him and even so. Tom swallowed and waited for her to speak. Her face was vague and she did not look at him when she spoke, her eyes wandered and wandered instead.

"The Rheas. The birds are big. The size of humans. They live on land. Too big to fly—"

She paused. Her brow crossed with confusion. She started again.

"A male Rhea has a dozen mates. He impregnates one bird and then moves on to the next. But he risks his life in defense of all his offspring."

She paused again. He had no idea what she was talking about. She shook her head.

"No. I wanted to tell you something different. Something about the Rheas."

She stopped and seemed to think about it. She picked loose a dry piece of skin from her lip.

"When the men fight to assert dominance it goes like this—"

She cleared her throat and closed her eyes.

"When the male Rheas fight to assert dominance it goes like this. They lock necks and spin around in circles. Because they are large birds—some as heavy as one hundred pounds— they gather tremendous momentum. They spin around and around and around. The one who gets dizzy first is the loser. They keep going until there is a loser. They don't stop until then."

She opened her eyes and smiled at him. Her face was cunning again, it was canny.

"Do you see?"

He did not see. He thought she might have lost her mind.

AFTER SHE TOLD the story about the Rheas, Tom began to think his father might marry the girl after all. The girl being the last remaining symbol of his power. The girl whom he would legitimate for this reason. It would happen the way a bank transfer happened. In material terms the ring would stay on her finger. Meanwhile the attachment it represented would transfer from one man to the other. It would be personally humiliating but Tom was used to being humiliated. He could have lived with it.

But this—he looks at the wagon. He watches his father check the ropes one last time. This abandonment, by all of them—it is worse than the nightmares that plague him at night. Jose leads three horses out from the stable. A pair to pull the wagon and his father's best horse. The old man mounts the expensive animal, the horse likely worth more than the farm at this point. He circles the wagon and goes to the girl, who has finished the tin of lobster. He takes the empty tin from her and hands it to one of the servants.

They are going. It is happening! It cannot be stopped. Nothing Tom can do will be enough to make the old man stay. Jose climbs aboard the wagon and whips the horses to life. They strain and pull and the wagon creaks. They move an inch and then a foot. The horses have never been made to carry such weight. Jose whips the pair again and at last they bear the wagon away. His father rides alongside. He does not look at his son as he goes.

Tom watches as the cart and horse move down the track. Two days ago his father had said to him—two days, it has only been two days, since his father announced that he was leaving. He had come to the shed, where Tom was cleaning the tack. It was dark and there were soft drifts of ash still on the floor and on the shelves.

"Thomas."

He had stopped at the sound of the old man's voice.

"We're going."

Carefully, he put down the bridle and harness.

"We—"

"Carine and I."

He turned to face the old man in the darkness. Both of them black from lack of light.

"Where?"

"To the city."

"For how long?"

"I do not know."

He nodded, his mouth was dry. He wondered why his father had chosen to speak to him here—in the shed, the smell of leather and oil and horse shit. Of all places.

"What will happen to the farm?"

"I leave that to you. It is yours, now."

The words were meaningless. The ownership was meaningless, now. Tom turned back to the bridle. He gripped the metal and leather straps. He picked up the rag, rubbed the oil into the straps, he polished the metal and tried to think of a way to speak.

"Is it because of the girl?"

The old man didn't answer. Tom continued to rub oil into the leather.

"It would be a shame—to let a woman come between us."

His voice catching. The words difficult to say. The old man still did not answer. Tom put the bridle down. He turned to face his father.

"I don't mind. I understand."

The old man did not move.

"You can have her."

He could not see the old man's face. He stood in the silence with his feet in the ash. The old man let out a short laugh. Like the muffled sound of heavy blows. Tom continued, raising his voice.

"There is no reason for you to leave. You could both stay. I understand."

The old man did not move. The silence bounded through the dark. Tom peered at him, hands trembling. He waited for the old man to speak.

"We are going."

Abruptly, his father turned. He walked to the door and pulled it open. The blood rushing to Tom's head as he watched. Standing in darkness, Tom watched the old man walk away. He tried to understand what had happened. What the old man had said. What he meant by what he said. How such a thing could be possible. He cleaned and oiled the bridles three times over. Then he trudged back to the house.

That was two days ago. Now Tom stands in front of the

house and watches as the procession—a short procession, very short—moves away. The girl's shawl flutters and then falls to her side. As the distance grows, he watches her small hand stroke it into place. He keeps watching, as the wagon pulls through the gate, down the track, becoming smaller and smaller. Then his father brings his own horse to a gallop, like he cannot wait to get away from the place. In a moment they are gone.

The servants stand stock-still. They stare after the wagon, down the track, like that will bring the old man back. Bring Jose back. They murmur to each other and wait. Celeste at the front of the group, peering hard at the horizon. They wait for the cart to return, for the miracle to happen. It is not going to happen. Tom wants to tell them this, he wants to tell Celeste, but they are not going to listen to him. There are still puffs of dust from the wagon visible on the road and he lets them cling to that.

Tom turns and goes back to the house. He is not aware that he is running but his feet are pounding the stone floor. The house is dark and cool. He turns and checks to see if anyone is following. Nobody is there, they are still standing at the front of the house, waiting for the old man to return. Tom wipes at the sweat on his forehead, he is suddenly perspiring, and continues down the dark hallway. He pushes open the door to the old man's study.

He scans the room, then heads to the desk. He opens the drawers, looking for papers, bank notes, bonds. Keys to the safe, sacks of money and coin. None of which he finds. He examines the walls, looking for a safe. He looks underneath the desk, below the tables. He shoves aside a painting on the wall—nineteenth century, a young woman and a small dog. The safe is empty as a drum.

He sits down. He thinks he must have fever—that must be the reason for the room spinning like it is. There are sicknesses in these parts. There is illness in his blood. Look at his mother. Now his father has deserted the farm, taken the money and the valuables, and Tom does not know where he has gone. He only knows that his father will set up a new life. The old man will have his third act.

And here is the son with nothing. The woman gone and the son's inheritance lost in a cloud of ash, carried away on a wagon cart. How will he make the farm run? How will he keep it safe? The joke is this: his father could save the farm but chooses not to. He built this place therefore it follows that he knows how to save it. But he chooses to go away instead. People will say it is about the unrest. They will say it is about the girl. They will say that the old man cannot bear the heat and has gone away instead.

It does not matter what people say. What matters is this: the old man has looked at the farm and decided it was not worth the trouble. It including Tom. The old man has made his choice and Tom has fallen by the wayside. When Tom has always believed, he has trusted in the bond between the land and the old man, he has allowed himself to think his place in that bond meant more than it did. He had thought the old man would take care of him.

Tom sits down in his father's armchair. The house is quiet. He looks at the papers that are scattered on the floor—he had upended drawers in his search. He picks up the papers again. There may be something he missed. Bank details. Offshore accounts. Hidden and electric treasure. He is not avaricious but he is human and practical despite himself. He stands up and goes to the desk. He looks at the papers—he reads them for the first time. He sets them down again.

He does not really understand. Tom does not have a head for such things. He is not accustomed to the idea of the world outside the farm. Tom has no inflated sense of his personal capacities, he is not unusually arrogant, but he believes his world will hold fast. The idea that changes in the world outside the farm—the idea of the world outside in the first place—that together they can shift his personal landscape, that is one, two, three leaps too many.

Tom does not know about appeasement. He does not know about the deals that are made. Expropriation is not a word in his small—small and shrinking, shrinking with each moment—vocabulary. He does not know that people can send you notices and the notices are not just pieces of paper but pieces of paper that have real meaning in the world.

Real meaning as in: I show you this piece of paper and you have one month to go. Real meaning as in: I show you this piece of paper and the property you think of as yours is no longer the property you think of as yours, the property you think of as yours is something else entirely.

According to the papers most of the land no longer belongs

to them. The papers (and the maps, there are many maps in amongst the papers) delineate the new acreage of the farm and it is dramatically reduced in size: the ten-mile spine has been lopped at both ends and only ten thousand acres remain. The negotiation has happened, the expropriation has begun. The land is being taken from the white settlers. The trees and hills have picked up and gone, they have packed their bags and departed down the track.

Like his father. They are gone in exactly the same way. Tom picks up a map indicating the new lay of the land and then drops it. It falls to the floor and crumples. Ninety thousand acres gone! He will need to ask his father what to do, only his father will know. But the old man is nowhere in sight. Instead there is just his signature, on the bottom of page after page after page.

His father is not moved by malice, Tom thinks, just by self-interest. His father being the most selfish man that ever breathed. For the first time Tom understands this. Only his mother was as selfish as the old man and that was why they did not love each other but were tied together in ways they half understood and fully resented. The two of them were the same in the end. They went in the same way. First the mother had gone by way of sea. Now the father has gone by way of land and the son is left alone.

Tom returns to the veranda. The servants have disappeared and the place is quiet. So here he is. The farm is his at last. He looks out to the horizon and he is terrified. The world outside, beyond its borders. He sees the three men and the documents they were examining. He sees his father reading the newspaper. The knotted grip of his hands. Tom has always been slow to understand. The men were not there because of what happened to the girl that night. The men only being messengers for something else. It had nothing to do with her. No man ever stayed because of what happened to a woman.

They stayed for other reasons. And now they are gone and the land is also gone. All that is left is the papers. The papers and with them the people who will come to claim the land. How will it happen? Who will come? Tom's laughter pierces through the air. The world is shrinking to a piece of paper. A white sheet pinned to the line and the sound of it thwacking against the wind. The land will cave. The paper is going to tear. And him, still here.

part two
The Forest

6

There were six barns on the farm. They were simple structures. A knocked together wood frame, covered in sheets of metal. Each barn had a plastic gutter along the roof to let off water when it rained. The six barns stood in the middle of fields and were spread across the property. Inside were bales of hay, tools and spools of wire fencing.

The spools of wire were taken first. Then the shelves were emptied of their tools. These items were lifted in the night and carried away. Their only trace being footprints in the grass and tracks from where the spools had been rolled. The barn door carefully closed behind them.

A week later the bolts were knocked out and the doors disappeared. The barns stood with their entrances gaping, six barns spread across the property without a door to lock or close. The barns circulated air. Nobody took notice. There was a hush. It was long and extended. It was exactly two weeks before the windows disappeared.

They were glass and therefore valuable. For these they

came with gloves and dirty quilts, into which they packed the panes as they knocked them from the frames. They returned for the frames the next day, having realized that these were also necessary. They cut them out with saws and went away by daylight, carrying the wood tucked beneath their arms.

The gutters were next to go. The plastic pipes were pulled down from the roofs and carried away. Then sheets of corrugated metal were dismantled and vanished square by square. Holes appeared in the barn sides. Entire walls were lifted away. Eventually each of the six barns was reduced to a bare wood frame. Like skeletons with the flesh burned away.

Finally even the frames went. The wood—some of it rotten with age and damp—was taken, along with scraps that had been abandoned in the grass. Hinges and bits of metal hardware. After a brief pause, the nails were also stolen up, gathered in their palms. They were secreted away until all that stood in place of the barns were stacks of hay. These rotted in the rain.

That was the prelude, which took place in the month following the land reform announcement. Which was broadcast on the radio and published in the newspaper, the news of it spreading like water. The whites being expulsed from the land in so many inches of ink and paper. The land shifting alliance across radio waves.

Then came the thing itself. He saw them through the window. Coming with their single wagons and mules, a tide of rusty instruments. The first thing they did was mark out boundaries with the barbed wire and wood from the barns.

Dozens of parcels, one not to be confused with the other. A hundred people colonizing their own land in a fever.

The land bent and buckled under the weight of the new men. They overturned the earth in a churn of activity, demonstrating how property was the thing most worshipped in the country. This being the first legacy of the white settlers. This being what the natives had learned.

He had dismissed most of the natives in the days following the announcement. There remained only a few dozen. These natives watched as pell-mell the farms went up on the hills around them. Each new farmer was given three cows and five sheep and a burlap sack of seed with which to start operations. The soil, now rich with ash, was plowed and the seed dumped into the ground. The livestock corralled into the corners of the plots and the houses hammered together with the weathered squares of corrugated metal.

In all the effect was—not what they were used to, and not especially felicitous. The natives shook their heads. They could leave the farm and put their names down for their acre and their three cows. Others had done so. But they decided against it. They were hedging their bets. They were waiting for something more, and did not believe this was the end of the matter.

THE OLD MAN returned six months later. Tom sits on the porch. It has been one month since the old man's return and still Tom calls it the porch in his head, what was once referred to as the veranda. There have been many retractions in his life, the most

93

important taking place in his head. It is now spring but there are shadows from inside the house and Tom is sitting on the edge of a pool of darkness.

There is nothing cheering to see in his face. Tom has been neutered by age and disillusion. His body is still young—he can run and jump with the best of them, he can move quickly when he has to, having always been good at running, in multiple senses of the word—but his face is like an old man already dead. His world has shrunk down to a fraction of its original size and he has already grown used to it.

After the land reform announcement, Tom was alone. The land was, for the time being, safe. The farm was his and he could do with it as he wished. But this farm was different from the farm he had envisioned, the farm he had filled his days imagining. He was forced to accept the reduced state of affairs, the missing father and the missing land being one and the same, both having gone at the same time, under the same circumstances.

The missing father being in two parts: the simple physical absence and the more difficult absence of the idea. The image of the father. Which was now gone, which had crumbled in front of him. The second being the greater loss. Having lost so much, Tom was obliged to divest himself further. He dismissed most of the servants and farm hands; others left of their own accord. He did not think to ask where they were going. He sold one thing and then he began selling all of it. He took whatever was offered, not knowing how to bargain.

He sold the motorboats. The tractors and the plows. (There

was a lot of machinery. It took a lot of machinery to maintain all that land. The storehouses containing piles of hardware and tools, the ossuary of the farm as it once was.) It was not hard. His attachment was to the land, not the apparatus it came with, and the valley was crawling with new farmers. The carpetbaggers bought the equipment in bulk and sold it at premium. Everything went except the fish farm, which continued to sit in a shed adjacent to the river, covered by a sheet of tarpaulin.

The other sheds went with the land. Tom did not know who owned them. The redistribution process had been fast and loose. It had seemed chaotic. Tom did not know if the result was what they wanted, if they have been satisfied by their gains. He did not even know who they were—communists, he heard, who did not believe in individual property. But then he heard that they were not communists after all but revolutionary capitalists. Nihilist rebels. None of these words meant anything to him.

Tom sat on the land that was still his. He had retained just enough natives to make the farm run. He had a little bit of money. But mostly he had erased himself from the land with his usual ease of retreat. And it was a good thing he had moved so fast. One week before the men arrived he sold most of the cattle. Then he saw them striding in from the distance—the same men, the three from before. Who had walked away and now came back. He was waiting for them when they arrived. They came on foot, their trousers coated in dust and their hands clutching stones in their pockets.

He didn't ask them in. He saw no reason to. They arrived and told him what he already knew. They took out the papers and presented them to him—he could tell, from the manner of presentation, that they expected no resistance from him. The old man's signature was incontestable. He acknowledged the papers. He told them he understood. He only wanted them to go away. Still they insisted on explaining the matter to him:

The violence had been spreading across the country for months. Then, a sudden escalation. It appeared the unrest had a leader. Someone capable of organizing the unrest into a movement. There was rumor of an illegal shipment of weapons—steps had to be taken to prevent chaos from claiming the country. Demands were made and agreed to. The Land Reform Bill was hurried through by the Government in a matter of days.

The men had been aware of the sea change for some time. For months they had been telling the old man that expropriation was looking more and more inevitable. However, there were opportunities in the chaos. The old days were gone and the Government was now fighting to maintain power. The whites were. That was a reality like the rest of it. But there were things to be gained, even in a time of attrition.

For example. They themselves had played their cards carefully and were subsequently appointed Special Commissioners to the Land Reform Process. They had told his father there were opportunities, even for men like them. As for a man like his father—well. It had been an awkward conversation. The old man had not taken it very well. He had not believed in their authority, even when they showed him the stamped and authorized papers. He had not wanted to believe in the changing times.

Granted, they hadn't known very much about how it would shake down. They didn't know very much now! They were still working out the details, it was a complicated thing, they had told the old man he would have some time before they seized the land. Of course, Tom would know all this already. His father would have told him. They had not realized Tom was due to inherit so soon—if they had, they would have included him in the conversations.

As it was, they were impressed by how quickly Tom had retrenched. They had not expected it. But here he was. Already off his land and one week before the deadline. He was as quick as his father, in his own way. It had been clever of him to sell the livestock. Unfortunately they were obliged to seize assets such as livestock and machinery along with the land—but here they were and there was nothing to take.

It had been chaos across the valley. They could tell him a story or two. As for Tom—they supposed he would find the adjustment quite easy. It was only land in the end. They had hardly been using it. Their herd having been so much reduced in recent years. Yes, he told them. That much was true. They had used the river. The river was how they had lived. They asked him what he planned to do now and he shrugged.

He thanked the men for coming. They were grinning, they clearly thought he was a fool. The idiot son tricked by the cunning father. Tom knew that was how they saw him. The men took out a pen and told him to sign some documents. Acknowledging the transfer of land. Exactly what his father had already agreed to, nothing more. He signed the papers without looking and then asked if they would excuse him, he had not been feeling well, not since his father had left.

The men told him they understood and left without another word. They went backward down the track and he watched them go from inside the house. Having locked the door behind them. The men left a copy of the papers inside with one of the servants. Nobody ever looked at the papers. Tom went to his bedroom, now in the servants' quarters (they had shut down whole wings of the house). He lay down in bed with an ice pack on his forehead.

He lay in bed and around him the business of the last forty years fell apart. The history of the farm dissolving. The mythology of the father crumbling at the knees. It was like picking a loose thread, it was like leaning back. He rocked onto his heels, he balanced on the back legs of his chair. He tilted and it came apart. The land and the old man, the first settler's claim across the sea. Then his mother, next came his mother, before the neighboring farmer and the fish, the churn of the river and the nets spread thick in the water.

In the dark room, he lay on his back, clutching the threads to his chest. He gripped them like a stuffed toy. When he was a child he spent days alone in the sickbed. The servants tended to his physical needs and nothing more. His mother was absent. His father also absent. The room was stuffy and dusty and the indifference gathered around him like a cloud. He would wish for the illness to prolong itself. To be left alone where he could not be seen.

And now it had happened. The old wish had been granted. It was like the sickness had taken over the world and so he lay, abandoned and forgotten. He dreamed—of a life that would not happen. The riding lodge he would set up, the wife he would marry, the tourists that would return to the farm. His dreams unfolded into the still air and overlapped. He had fever and the sheets grew musty and he broke into frequent and profuse sweats.

Tom retreated into his bedroom, into his inertia, and the farm—what was left of it, ten thousand acres and almost no river front—ran itself. The small herd of cattle rounded in and out. The garden tended. He lay in bed and his dreams multiplied as he watched the hill crawl with new life. Hardly knowing if it was hallucination or not. He sank into the land. The separation from the earth always less distinct for Tom than for his father. The separation giving way even now, although the land no longer wanted him.

Tom's respite was temporary. There was no real comfort in it and soon he was spat back into the world. His solitude had not lasted any more than a matter of months. The world—as it was and as it had been, both came crowding back in. The country returning. Linear time alongside it. The earth shuddering and the world outside raging with change. The old structures of power returned but in altered form. And now his life is both the same and entirely different.

Tom stands up. He goes into the kitchen to find Celeste. She is at the stove. Always she is at the stove. For six months she had walked the land (the farm was diminished but it was still big enough for walking). As if she were looking for Jose and the old man. As if she thought she might find them, somewhere on the land. Now she is back at the stove and Tom thinks she is both relieved and reassured. Despite the changes that have taken place, that are still taking place.

She nods to him as he comes in. She is making soup for the old man. A one-dish meal. Before she cooked for the extended household. Lavish meals for a full table. It goes without saying that the menu has changed, but this is not just because of their reduced circumstances.

"Is it almost ready?"

She grunts. She shields the stove from him with the broad surface of her back.

Fine, he thinks. That is fine. She can make the soup but the soup can go nowhere without him. That is his job. Not that it is a job he especially enjoys.

He has a series of disconnected thoughts. They do not represent the best aspects of the man. He feels wary. He feels hard done by. He knows this is a petty feeling. He is tired. He is surprised that in most ways it is still life as he knows it. He eats the same food. Sleeps in the same bed. Shits the same shit. Yes. All of this being true and also not true.

He watches Celeste crouching over the pot. Stirring with her long-handled wood spoon. She is not used to this kind of cooking. It is not her strength or what she likes. Her strength is something else. Rich sauces. Charred meats (crisp and smoky on the outside, meltingly tender inside). Butter and cream and wine.

Not this. Vegetable broth thinned with water. No salt but mixed with one part chicken stock because she cannot resist— she does not work with a stock made solely of carrots and onions, what is the point of it. Nothing good ever came of bad food. Who ever got better off bad food? Who was ever cured?

He ignores her. (She does not actually say this aloud, she says all this to him with her back, which remains hunched over the pot. She has slipped in a little cream, although he has said not to. Although he has told her this only makes matters worse. He understands that she cannot help it. She does not know how else to tend to the old man.) Tom walks around so that he can see the pot. And the soup inside, which looks cooked.

"The soup is ready. And Celeste. No butter on the toast this time."

She glares at him and shakes in salt and pepper. With a wave of open palm. She adds more cream, as he watches. He shakes his head. He wonders if this will continue. If she will persist in seeing battles where they aren't. She is still glaring at him when she reaches for the loaf of bread. She seizes a bread knife and saws off two slices. These she slips into the wire grill and props over the open fire.

He checks the tray while they wait for the bread to toast. The soup does not smell especially fragrant but he is hungry and it reminds him of this fact. He slices a piece of bread and eats it absent-mindedly. It is a little stale. Celeste looks at him disapprovingly.

"I would have toasted it for you."

He waves the statement away. Mouth too full for talking. He checks the tray and is careful not to spray any bread crumbs. Can't be careful enough. He checks: the spoon and knife and fork. Resting on the cloth napkin lining the tray. Everything looks fine. He rests his hands on the tray and then is overwhelmed. To think of picking up the tray and carrying it away. He removes his hands from the tray and sits down, suddenly in need of rest. Celeste looks up.

She pulls the grill from the fire and pries it open. She flips the pieces of toast onto the cutting board and severs them in two. Then she wraps them in a cloth and sets them on the tray. She eyes him as she reaches for the butter.

"No butter, Celeste."

She ignores him as she cuts a square.

"No butter, Celeste."

She thrusts the butter dish back and wipes her hands on her apron. Reaches for a bowl and serves a single ladle. Places it carefully on the tray. She looks at him.

"I can take it in."

"That isn't necessary."

She looks at him cunningly.

"You look tired. Stay here. This time I will take it in. For once I can take it in."

"No."

"You will become exhausted. I am telling you."

102

"It's okay."

He rises and looks at her. She is right. He is tired. He will become exhausted. Everything she is saying is right. But she cannot take the tray in. They both know this. He picks up the tray. She makes a noise of protest but does nothing to stop him. He checks for the saucer with the pill. Yes. It is there. Tucked in beside the napkin. Now he lifts the tray carefully so that the soup, the glass of water, will not spill. He picks it up, exits the kitchen, and disappears down the hall.

7

The room is dark. The old man lies in the bed and thinks about the things he needs to do. He can hear noises outside the wall and windows. The noises of the farm. He makes lists in his mind and they grow—down the page, grow in all directions. Run to the side and go off the edge and he is overcome. He cannot keep them from growing. On certain days he can feel the lists on his skin. Crawling across his chest, down his legs, into the interior of his body. This causes the twitching and the spasms.

There is some confusion in his mind. He does not understand what is happening to him. On a bad day he will understand that something new is taking place, that his body is sailing toward uncharted territory. But even on a bad day he does not understand what that means. His mind will not allow it. His mind is crumbling, it is eroding into sand, but it is still the strongest thing about him.

The old man grips handfuls of sand, he remembers that he has been growing old for a long time, that he grows old and grows stronger. He grows and around him people cave and it is almost like they want to. That is his secret. It has not always been like this. When he was young he had struggles and the world did not conform to his wishes. Then he grew old and the world started giving in to him and then it continued, it gave and it gave.

But now the world is defying him again. Shrinking, spiraling, and he does not understand why. The world is taking it back! First it was the country. The land changing, the property retreating, beyond his power, outside his jurisdiction. Then the girl, failing him as she did, her body occupied by another man's seed. He tried to open the world, he tried to clamp it down so it would stay and instead he was compelled to come back. He—of all people—he had been forced to retreat into a corner, the girl stumbling behind him, and the corner not even safe.

His head twitches in a spasm that he cannot control. His body is defying him like the world is. The world being in his body as the world shrinks down. As it sits in his swollen belly like a ball. Apart from that there are his legs and his chest and his arms. That is all that is left. Even that is going, even that will be gone if he is not careful. He would like to put his body back together. He thinks about joining the bones and muscles and making them strong again.

He crouches on the edge of the bed. He is a collection of bones, a belly like a fruit pit and limbs like shards. His arms splintering at the touch. He cannot believe this body belongs to him. He is not sure that it does. He tries to do arm exercises.

105

He lifts his arm to the height of his shoulder and back down again. After two lifts he cannot breathe and needs to lie down. He leans against the bedpost and grips it with both hands. He levers himself down to the bed. Then he peels his hands from the bedpost and presses them to the sheet. The air rattling in his throat.

He lies in bed and waits. He closes his eyes, but his mind does not rest. He sleeps—people tell him that he is sleeping well, they tell him it is good to rest, that he needs it. But he wakes up exhausted from dreams he cannot remember, he wakes and he does not feel refreshed as he has always felt refreshed. He dreams and the dream is as intense as hallucination. But never as intense as the pain, which is nothing but unbearable sensation. Which is bound only to get worse.

So he lies in bed in terror but nobody would guess it. Never underestimate the charisma of the dying. It has attached itself to the old man. Who grows bigger and bigger with it. He spreads across the farm, that is still shrinking from expropriation, that is still being cut down to size. He seizes hold of the house and land. He refuses the transfer of ownership. But he alone knows, can see, what is coming.

The door opens and Tom enters with the soup. The old man opens one eye and watches him as he sets the tray on the table by the bed. Tom lifts his father up and props him on pillows. He reaches for the cloth napkin and carefully unfolds it. He spreads the cloth down to the old man's swollen belly. It is hard as a rock and getting harder by the day. Tom sets a chair beside the bed, he picks up the bowl of soup and feeds him.

106

When the old man returned to the farm one month ago, he was on his own two legs. The unfamiliar car—scraped and sputtering as it was—came down the track and the old man sat in the back. The girl sat beside him, and up in front Jose looked not like a driver and not like a farmhand either. The car window rolled down and the old man peered up at him.

"There have been changes."

Tom nodded. Here, too, he wanted to say. Here, too, there have been changes. It is not the same as how you left it. He was filled with anger and relief. Don't come back / come back. The father's face a complicated thing as it peered up at him from inside the car. That the old man thought he could return and find it unchanged. As if nothing had happened. As if he had nothing to do with the nothing that had happened. He would like to tell his father about his resentment, his life-time of resentment, now coming to a head and barely understood. I have things to tell you, he thought. There are things you need to hear.

There was no opportunity for that. Later that afternoon his father collapsed. He fell six feet something down to the ground. The girl crying for help. The domestics running. They picked him up and carried him to the settee.

He was shivering from cold and they covered him with a blanket. There was blood on the tiles and blood on the old man's head. They could hear his teeth chattering inside his skull. The old man lay on the settee and tried to recover and vomited twice onto the floor. The girl stood and stared, hands on her belly. Her condition also changed. It has been like this, she said. It is getting worse.

The old man looked ill. His color was wrong. His body slipped out from under the cover—an ankle and a calf and both like sticks. Tom had never seen his father so thin, he would not have thought it possible. He turned and told one of the boys to prepare a bedroom, close to the kitchen and their quarters, where it would be easy for them to tend to the old man.

The old man heard but did not protest. He closed his eyes. The sharp smell of vomit on the air. He said to Tom that he had not been well and had come back to the farm to get better. He had come here to recover. Tom only nodded. He said the farm was not as he had left it. The old man had closed his eyes and did not respond. Tom said that things had changed here, too. I have changed. The old man still did not respond. Tom did not say anything further.

They set up three rooms for the old man. A sitting room, a study, a bedroom. The girl slept in the sitting room. The old man slept in the bedroom. He sat on the porch during the day and the girl took him on short walks. They went out across the lawn and then she would tell him he was tired. No, he would say. No. I am not tired. You are, she would tell him. And he would ignore her, but soon they would return to the house.

In this way a perimeter was established. The old man took meals in the sitting room and he spent hours in the porch's thin spring sun. He did not regain his health. He grew thinner instead. His color went to gray and then it went to green. In certain lights, at certain times of the day. In other circumstances it returned to its usual gray. He was constantly shifting and they were losing him in the change.

The perimeter, once established, shrank rapidly. One week and he could no longer go on his morning walk. Another week and he was staggering as he made his way to the porch. He lurched from wall to furniture as he made his way across the hall. He would sit speechless for half an hour as he recovered but he would not accept their help.

Then the old man gave up the porch and stayed in his rooms. Once his father owned everything as far as he could see. Now it was three rooms and even those rooms would go. He gave ground—each foot, every inch, signaled what was coming. It was in this way that Tom realized the old man was dying. Animals died in the same way. Their territory taken away. Cattle retreating into their stalls. Wild dogs cowered in a corner. The look of it indistinguishable.

Death equalized everything. Tom saw but did not believe the old man was dying. The confusion proof that Tom was not prepared for the end that was coming. He disavowed the knowledge, the thought like a dry seed in the palm. He clenched his fist and tried to hide it, he buried it in his back pocket. Where it sat suspended, alongside his rage toward the old man and all that he had done, the old man's fall from grace.

A pocket full of confusion. Tom concentrates on the present. He thinks that is how he will get through this—and he is not even sure, he could not say, what "this" is. He sits beside his father. He spoons soup into his mouth. Two days ago the old man decided to accept help. He had no real choice in the matter. He could no longer satisfy his body's basic functions without it. In this he chose Tom, who counts for nothing and is therefore fit for the job. The old man is loath to be seen by the natives in a state of weakness. Whereas being seen by Tom is like being seen by no one at all.

So Tom now has the privilege of being intimate with his father and this is something new, something that once would have meant a great deal to him. For example, he now sits beside his father's bed. Close enough to see the texture of his skin. The individual hairs on his arm. Close enough to smell the stench of his breath, which is stronger than he imagined. Tom brings the spoon to the old man's mouth and obediently he opens. Both of them ignoring the obedience like it never happened.

The door opens. The girl comes in and he nods to her. She walks with effort. (Laboriously is the only word and not only because of her condition. It is not a felicitous pregnancy. It has aged her, it has drained her of life. Although she is still slim and sly, and that despite the bump.) She hobbles to a chair against the wall and sits down. The old man swallows the food in his mouth. He opens his eyes and looks at the girl.

She sits in the chair like she is pinned against the wall. Aware as she is of the old man's animosity. Tom spoons soup into his father's mouth and the old man continues to watch the girl. Who would like to make herself small but cannot because of her belly. Who shrinks and shrinks back even as the belly remains. It is its own thing, it just happens to be attached to her body. They are all aware of this.

Tom looks at the bowl of soup. It is mostly eaten. He dips a piece of toast into the bowl and pushes it into his father's mouth. He opens and chews and swallows. His eyes still on the girl. Tom picks up the tray and turns to go. He looks at the girl and motions in the direction of the door. She does not move. He looks at her again and reluctantly she stands and follows him.

They close the door behind them and look at each other. Without saying anything she reaches for the tray. Her fingers push over his and she yanks the tray to her so that the dishes rattle. He lets her take it. Her touch on his touch. She holds the tray so that it rests on her belly. Then she turns and goes, the empty tray sitting heavy on her pregnancy.

He looks after her. Eight months pregnant and that is the other thing that came home in the car. Showing, showing— her belly strains at the seams of her dress. Each day she splits another dress and must sew together a new one. The girl is still tiny and the pregnancy is unnatural. Every time her dress splits Tom expects to see a plastic belly, a padded pillow, a not truth in the shape of a truth. But there is nothing but stretched flesh, an acreage of flesh in her belly.

His father dying but still capable of engendering life. Capable of colonizing a woman's body. He is a man after all. Tom is also a man but of these things he knows nothing. When he first saw the girl's belly he had been overcome with jealousy.

The jealousy being in several parts, the girl's belly further proof of his displacement, further proof also of the old man's obscenity.

But Tom was not altogether correct in his assessment. Which means that he was not prepared when the reversal took place. He should have been. After all there was a precedent. A man can be dying but he does not change his behavior. This man in particular, this old man—he becomes more himself as he goes, he simply distills himself as he dies. His power going nowhere.

The night they returned, the three of them—his father, the girl and himself—sat down to dinner. For months Tom had subsisted on rice and beans. But that night Celeste made a heroic effort and the table was only two or three—maybe four—times removed from what it used to be. Succulent cuts of meat and fish. Tom had not seen a fish cooked or alive for months.

When the first dish arrived the old man said, "I have missed your cooking, Celeste." He took a bite and she blushed and bustled her way back into the kitchen. But he did not finish the terrine or the soup or the courses that followed. He said that he was not hungry. They had been on the road for nearly a week. Tom nodded and said his room was prepared, he could go to bed, whenever he liked.

Only his father did not want to go to bed. He drank his port (A month ago he was drinking! A month ago he was able to sit through a meal) and stared across the table at his son. Then he announced that the girl would give birth in two months' time.

Tom nodded. In his head he was doing the math: nine minus seven is two is six months minus seven is one month. The old man said preparations should be made.

Then his eyes slid to the girl, who looked at him blankly. She opened her mouth as if to say something. Her lips pursed but no sound came out. The old man looked at her sharply. A little later he stood up and said he was going to bed. The girl stood up with him. Her arm snaking around his. She said they could make their way alone. She said she would take care of things.

Tom cleared the table. Now that he had dismissed most of the servants the cleaning was left to him. He didn't mind. He had become used to it, it had taken him no time to become used to it. He carried the plates, the silverware, the wine glasses. Celeste had uncorked a bottle from nowhere. Perhaps she had whole crates of wine hidden beneath the stairs—clearly there were things happening in this house that he did not know about. He put on one of Celeste's aprons and washed the dirty dishes.

He was taking the apron off when the girl came back into the kitchen. He struggled with its knots and flaps before yanking it off at last.

"Yes?"

"A cup of tea."

He nodded and reached for the kettle. He filled it with fresh water and struck a match against the gas range.

"No," she said.

"No," he repeated.

"Sit down."

She was trying to sound like she had a handle on the situation. She did not have a handle on this or any situation, and they both knew it. Her lips cracked. Her face was tired. And yet he was helpless, though he did not feel tenderness toward her. Her presence confusing to the man. She blinked and leaned against a chair. He sat down.

"Your tea."

She shook her head.

"I will turn the stove off."

She shook her head again. He listened to the flame whirr behind them.

"This baby."

"Yes."

"Please don't act as if it has nothing to do with you."

The kettle was boiling. He stood and switched the gas off.

"Everything here has to do with everything else."

He looked at her. He tried to sound reassuring. Although he himself did not feel reassured.

"We will make the preparations."

"That is not what I mean."

He sat down uneasily. She leaned forward.

"Don't you want to know who the father is?"

"That does not concern me. That is between you and him."

"You honestly don't remember?"

She had arranged her features into a mask of anger and incredulity but did not appear to be feeling either of those emotions. She sat down next to him and folded her hands across her belly.

"You were drunk."

He shivered.

"I don't drink."

"And yet you were very drunk. I was frightened when you knocked on my door. You could barely walk straight. It was over very quickly."

"That's impossible."

"Your father was surprised when I told him but then he said it was as it should be."

She has not recovered her mind, he thought. Her mind cracked back there and she has not recovered the pieces. She cannot think he will believe this story. She cannot think that he will be so foolish. He of all people. The old man's son. And yet she continued to talk.

"I understood," she said. "You were—you are, my fiancé."

He blinked.

"You have certain rights."

She was watching him carefully. He told himself not to listen to her. He reminded himself that she was full of deceit. But the idea—no, not an idea but a collection of urges and images, of the girl, and the farm, of a version of life—had been seeded inside him once more. There could be other children, for example. He reminded himself that he had never touched her, though not for lack of want. His mouth was dry like she had stuffed it with cotton.

"I have rights—"

She nodded. He did. Though she was not going to open herself up for him, this shop being closed for business, however temporarily. His rights being granted too late. But there was no reason for her to tell him this. After all, it was self-evident. He stared at her and wet his lips. A crease of confusion appeared across his forehead.

"What is it you want?"

SHE LOOKED AWAY and after a second shook her head. She did not know what she wanted. The measure of what she wanted had been taken away. The tape having been stolen. It had been no easy thing—keeping the pieces from floating away. It had taken everything she had. If she'd had an endless amount of string she would have tied them together and then been whole again but as it was sometimes the splitting came back to her in a flash.

She looked around the kitchen. And now the growing inside her. Which she had avoided all these years by cunning and tact but was now a definite reality. Her body grew heavier each day like the baby was made of lead. The chain tightening. Her world also shrinking. Just like it did for the old man. In this they were also the same. Their bodies revolted in unison and the world around them—

She stood up and went to the stove and turned the gas back on under the kettle. She waited for the water to boil while Tom stood beside her. She was not imagining a life with this man: that was not the way she thought about it. She only needed him to do what he was meant to do, do as the old man said he would. He had made her a promise. He had not spoken the words, it was in no way binding, but it was the best that she had.

She stared down at the flame. The sickness had clenched her head and stomach. The first wave came just days after they reached the city. She felt her insides shift but thought that was to be expected. Given what had taken place. Given what had been inserted and then torn out. Then she was late and she still didn't think. She was trying to recover all the pieces of her body. It never occurred to her that something could grow in such a desert.

It was not a good time for such a thing. She was in no condition for growth. While her head was still retrenching and her body. There had been lasting damage. She half expected the baby to fall out of her but it did not. She half expected the baby to curdle inside her but it did not. She tried to help it. Twice she tried, but it insisted on living, on thriving inside her. She therefore needed protection. The old man had stood by her thus far. Now she was pregnant and she had to guess if he would continue to stand by her.

Even if the child was not his. Which she believed it was not. She spent a long time going over the math and the thing was never entirely certain—scribble on paper and count your fingers, give or take a day, it was hard to know. The father remained faceless and nameless like the group of men that night. The father was a many-headed monster and that was the truth. As for what was growing inside her—there weren't prayers sturdy enough for that.

She went to the old man and told him what was currently

transpiring inside her guts. She waited for him to ask if he was the father and to tell him yes, to assure him of course yes, obviously yes, who else? But the question never came. He asked her why she did not get rid of it and she told him that she had tried. She had tried, she had tried to get rid of the damn thing but she had failed and now she was stuck. It was tied around her neck like a weight.

Then there was rage in his face. This man, who could bear her rape but not the evidence of it. Who could not live with the evidence growing up in front of him. She half thought he might tell her to leave. But he did not. Because he was sick, they soon realized that he was sick and would need to journey back to the farm. Things had not gone according to plan. They had run out of money and the old man had discovered that no bank would extend him credit. They had already sold the horses and jewels.

He said there was nowhere else for him to go. He could not stay in the city. She said to him the country did not feel safe. She said she did not believe in the peace. There had been rumors that the violence was spreading across the country again. That the natives had not been appeased. The Government had not done enough. She asked if there was not another way, another option. He stared at her and then told her not to believe in idle gossip.

He would have left her if he could. His old use for her being gone. But he could not travel alone. She therefore tried to make herself useful. Driven as she was by need. She made preparations for their departure. In haste they purchased a car—she handed Jose a wad of bills and two hours later he returned with a Buick built like a hearse and some rusted canisters of gas. A joke contraption that would break as the wheels turned. It was not worth discussing. They packed their bags into the car and left in the morning.

Jose drove them through the traffic in the city. As soon as they reached the autoroute he gunned the motor and they shot down the empty road. However, it was full of potholes and invisible ditches. They punctured two tires and the motor repeatedly stalled. They were constantly stopping and coaxing—coaxing and beating, they alternated between the two—the hearse into movement again.

By that time the girl had grown desperate to reach the farm and the enclosure of land. She was nervous and the open road terrified her. Meanwhile, the old man was so sick they could not get south fast enough and she saw that they were returning to the farm for him to die. He lay in the backseat and expired by the mile. He was green and blue and sweating from the journey. The girl was no great shakes either. Nausea meant she spent half the trip with her head out the window as they drove, hurling her guts out or trying to.

Halfway to the valley she made Jose stop the car and she vomited onto the side of the empty road, so much she thought she must have heaved the baby out. As she stumbled back to the car she turned to see if there was a fetus dropped in with the half-digested protein and starch. Once inside the car, she shouted at Jose to go. They screeched away down the road and she would have told Jose go faster if she'd glimpsed a little fist, a little foot, waving out of the puddle of mush.

They were a hundred miles from the farm when the old man rose up from the backseat. Like a vampire—he rose up from the sleep of his coffin, having been supine the whole of the journey, and said to the girl, "You will tell Thomas about the child." She turned to look at him. She would tell him what? That he was going to have a brother?

She said this hopefully. She reminded herself that she was as strong as the old man. That under different circumstances she could have owned and run her own farm. That she was more like the old man than either cared to admit. He shook his head. "A son. You will tell him that he is going to be a father." Then he lay back down.

The father's shame transferred to the son. These being men made up of appearances. Now she stood in the kitchen and waited for the kettle to boil. Tom stood by the table and watched. He had spent a lifetime under the weight of the old man. His endurance was considerable. He was like one of those hardy plants that grew low and close to the ground. You didn't notice them but they outlived the taller and more verdant ones. Yes, probably he would be here when she was all but been and gone. She watched him shift and scrabble his eyes across the floor.

She told him to sit down. She no longer felt afraid. She believed that he would fall in line. In the same way she had. She would have her security. It was the old man. He overcame them both but it was more than that. The truth was that there was too much else. The country was in turmoil. And there was besides: sickness and growing and dying. How could they do anything but give in, to what was obvious, rather than what was good? In the face of that accumulation.

Yes. Even she. She looked at Tom. She felt a stir of sympathy despite herself. The gap between them lessening by a sliver. She wanted to tell him that there were some things they held in common. She wanted to say they were not entirely different. This was against her better judgment. The thin edge of the wedge.

8

Tom and the girl sit in the kitchen. Tom leans forward. If the old man dies that will be one thing, he tells her. But what if he recovers and lives? His father looks out the window and does not seem to see the change in the land. He talks to Tom about what they will do next year. He tells him about the improvements that must be made. They will open the fish farm once the water runs clear, they will add another pool, they will open up new trails, maybe a second lodge.

Tom does not think the old man sees the change in the country or the change in his own body. Tom does not try to convince him otherwise. He does the opposite. It is like playing a game of charades. He tells and he does not tell, he does not see why he should do either. The image of the father is gone, but Tom is still afraid of him. Afraid for him. That part of the relationship remaining intact. Tom drinks his tea and asks the girl how much the old man knows, how much he remembers.

She shrugs. He knows plenty, she tells him. He knows more than you know, more than you and me put together. He tells her this cannot be the case. He asks if she has been listening to what he has been saying.

She shakes her head. You have known him forever. How can you know him so little? He is lying in the bed but there is nothing weak about him. He is lying in the bed and he is going but until he is gone the old man is still there. Do you understand?

He understands. He looks at the girl. He becomes more attached to her by the day. Also to the child growing in her belly. Toward whom he feels proprietary. His idea of what life will look like after the old man's death being tied up in the woman, also in the child that is not his own. She heaves her belly around the house and now she stops to catch her breath, she holds her belly in her hands like she is worried it will fall to the ground. Her skin is growing dull and her hair dry. She looks as if the child inside her is draining her of life, the growing child and the dying man.

Tom asks if she is getting enough to eat. If she is getting enough rest. He tells her she should try not to worry too much. She tells him that she is fine. Everything is fine. Thank you for asking. She knows that he is doing his best. His best is not good enough but she sees that it is something. They are beginning to grow tired. They are starting to be ground down by the old man's dying.

Both slept poorly the night before. The old man could not stop coughing and called to them continuously—for water, for light, for a goddamned cigar. The girl brought him one and then he ignored both her and the cigar. He is beyond cigars.

They know this. She knew this when she brought it to him and still she brought it to him. She allowed herself this. She thinks it must be hard for Tom, Tom who would not have brought the cigar and will therefore never be free.

She thinks: Tom does not know how to love the old man so he loves the land instead. She had seen this from the start. His emotion toward the old man unresolved. His feeling long misdirected. Even now, he would like to stay on the farm. In this house, in this room, at this table if possible. He clings to the land and the farm and really he is holding on to his father. Whom he hates and loves in equal measure. A wave of pity and she reminds herself that the problems of the farm have long been in place. Some of them too long to solve or change.

The girl leans forward.

"How much money is there?"

He looks up.

"Money?"

"Yes. Money. How much money is left?"

He shakes his head and looks blank. His expression is stupid, stupid without thought or pretense. Which cannot be right. The old man said there was more to Tom than met the eye. He said that Tom could be canny, on occasion. Good with money. Good with numbers. He had left the farm—not in good hands but in hands that would do. That was all he said. But the girl listened.

The girl listened and that is why she knows that Tom knows more than he is letting on. She believes this because she needs to. The old man will die. And then what will become of them?

She has staked a great deal on Tom's good hands. On the protection of the land, however reduced it may be. She sits with her knees apart to accommodate her belly, she sits back into her chair. She clears her throat to show she means business and takes a good long look at him.

"The money."

Tom appears startled by the sharpness in her voice.

"There is not much."

"How much?"

"Very little."

"What has happened to it?"

He shrugs.

"There was not that much to begin with. There was not money. There was land."

"How much land remains?"

"There are still some pastures."

The old man is wrong. His son is an idiot. He stares at her and does not know what he is saying. She leans forward.

"Tell me what is left."

"They took almost everything."

"Tell me what is left."

"Enough for a small farm. That is what we are. A small farm."

She can see that it pains him to say this. He is not without vanity. He is not a man without want. But that want is small and it is compromised, it has undergone a lifetime of atrophy. She sees that she will need to do the wanting for both of them. She leans back and looks at him. She wills her voice steady.

"But there is still land."

"Yes."

"And in what condition, since the eruption and the ash?"

He does not reply. He blinks and then wets his mouth.

"I haven't looked."

"Are the cattle able to pasture?"

"They tell me that it will be fine."

"Who tells you this?"

"The farmhands."

"Which ones?"

"The farmhands."

She looks at him and knows that he has no idea. It has been too much for him, he has not spent these past months drawing up business plans. There have been other things to worry about. Well and he has been through hell but so has she. She hoists herself to her feet, panic rising.

"We will go and look. Now."

"We can't leave him alone."

"Of course we can."

He licks his lips nervously.

"Right now we need to take care of him. We agreed, remember? That is what we need to do."

She shakes her head.

"I will wait for you at the stables. We will bring Jose."

She goes out into the hall and looks for Jose. Jose does not like her. She knows that he does not like or trust her. But he listens to her. He does as he is told. Having been the first to realize the old man was dying. The question is only this: who will come out on top? The son or the girl or the two together?

She can see the question vibrate inside him. He is armed with the instinct to survive and it is ugly, but then she herself is the same. The two of them understand each other.

She walks out into the entrance hall. From here she can see the other wings, the wings that have been closed, sitting in darkness, windows shuttered. She thinks about the old man's talk. He is half in delirium but is still more shrewd than the rest. It is not crazy to imagine there is money in the house. They would have to give up the cattle but they could take visitors, visitors who would fish and ride and pay like before, once sanity has been restored to the land. It is not impossible to think this might happen.

She quickens her pace as she leaves the hall. She reminds herself that she is looking for Jose.

She finds him outside. Tending the kitchen garden. Working over the pea shoots and the beets and the asparagus and the lettuces. Things that grow and that she knows nothing about. She stands in the garden in her robe and slippers and realizes how little they leave the house. It is warmer than she expected, well into spring. She watches Jose bend over the plants. She wonders who has told him to tend the garden, who has remembered to do that.

"Jose!"

He looks up when she calls and stands. To see what she wants.

"Yes."

"Tom and I are going to take a tour of the property. Do you know the new borders?"

He nods.

"Will you show us?"

He nods again.

"We will meet you at the stables in half an hour."

She returns to the house. She is a woman of imagination but it does not occur to her to wonder how much longer Jose will remain. How much longer Celeste and the farmhands will stay. Why they do not leave and start their own farm, claim their own acre of land. Their loyalty is taken for granted—by Tom, Carine, the old man. Its meaning never examined or perceived.

Back in the kitchen, Tom is still sitting at the table. The girl does not see what it is like for him. He understands this at once. She proposes a life, an idea of a life. But even as he grasps at it, the seed of his confusion grows heavy and unwieldy. He can feel that it is starting to sprout. She makes preparations for the future and the shoots press up around him, he worries about hiding them, he is certain that his father will spot the new growth any moment now. It is beyond his control, it cannot be suppressed. But this is not something he can explain to the girl, who would not understand, it is not even something he can explain to himself.

Tom goes back to the kitchen in search of Celeste. He finds her and tells her that they are going out. She asks him how long they will be gone and he thinks and then says that he does not know. He does not know how long it takes to circle the property because he does not know how big it is. It is the first time he has faced the concrete evidence—the physical borders—of the farm's contraction. Celeste asks him if the girl is going with him and he tells her that she is. She makes a sharp sound in her mouth to show him that she disapproves. He tells her that it was the girl's idea in the first place and then says they will go no faster than a walk, a trot, certainly not a canter or a gallop.

He turns and leaves, feeling like a fool. At the stables, the girl is already waiting. She sits on a rock with her arms wrapped around her belly. She looks like she has been sitting there for a long time. She looks up at him.

"Finally."

"I was speaking with Celeste."

She heaves herself up and looks at him without replying. He goes into the stables and she sits down again. Hands on her belly. The lead baby grows and it grows. She sits on the rock and she looks like she is about to roll over onto the ground.

Tom brings the horses out. With some effort they get her onto the mare and she grips the reins and the saddle and she looks secure enough. There is determination in her face. She urges the mare forward without waiting. Tom and Jose mount and then follow her out the stable yard.

They ride up the valley and across the fields. Tom has always favored the pasture but the farm is oriented to the river. The house looks to the river, the gate frames the river, the windows and the French doors and the veranda. In the direction of the fields there is no veranda or French doors and very few windows. When the old man drew up the specifications for the house he did not know about the day when they would have nothing but a pittance of river front to their name.

They ride and are silent. Tom sees the girl glare at him. She would like him to question Jose. She would like him to gather information about the fortunes of the farm, the state of their affairs. Tom is not prepared to do this, on some level he has not fully understood or accepted the reduction of the farm. He looks and does not know what is theirs and what is not. He sees lushness around him but has no idea what that lushness is worth, he does not know what they can hope to preserve.

He hesitates. Then he asks Jose how the cattle are faring. Jose rides ahead and speaks to him over his shoulder.

"They are fine, they are not bad."

"When will they take the herd to the auction?"

Jose shrugs.

"I do not think you should worry."

He does not elaborate. Jose never elaborates. They continue across the pasture in the direction of the hills. The girl is silent. Jose points to the edge of the field.

"That is the north border of the land."

They peer to where he points. It is in spitting distance. Tom fingers the reins.

"There?"

"There."

Jose turns and now they follow no path in particular, they meander across the fields. They trace the border of a piece of land that makes no sense. Jose points again and tells them this is the west border of the land. This is the east border of the land. He turns. The girl pulls up beside them and now she speaks.

"Where are the other fields?"

Jose shakes his head.

"There are no other fields."

"Tom showed me the map."

"The map is out of date."

The girl laughs and pats the mare on the neck.

"Impossible."

"But true."

"How?"

"The Government is becoming desperate. It is making more and more concessions. Each week there are announcements on the radio."

He looks at the girl. She turns pale. They have not listened to the radio since their return from the city and it has been one month, it has been longer. She grips the reins tighter but shakes her head defiantly.

"They cannot take away the land by announcements on the radio."

"Except they do."

"I don't believe you."

"The Land Reform Process has been a failure. The people are not satisfied. There is more and more violence in the country, only this time it is organized. This time it is armed."

He shrugs.

"It is like they predicted. The unrest is now a rebellion. They give away your land, but who knows if that will be enough."

The girl turns the mare around and gallops across the land that is no longer theirs. She goes as far as the top of the hills and then comes to an abrupt halt. From the top of the hills the land once stretched another five thousand acres. Now she is already trespassing.

Tom and Jose follow and then they also look down the slope. In the distance they can see the land is divided into a hundred tiny farms. Recently it had been empty. Now it is a complex diagram of fences and ownership that is difficult to decode. It is no longer taking place in their language. Still, one meaning of the landscape is clear to them. The girl stares down at the land and her eyes are filled with dread.

"Where did these people come from?"

"They are from here. Where else?"

"But how have they come so quickly?"

"The rebellion. It has organized the land. It is overseeing the process. The Government no longer has any power."

It turns out, Tom thinks. It turns out these are people who do not believe in property until it is theirs. Then it is defended tooth and nail. They will push back, Tom thinks. The momentum is on their side. It will carry them forward as they push and push. Until they will be pushed into the river for all he knows. The force of it being stronger than anything they have ever known.

The girl says that she is not feeling well. She backs the mare up and then she turns her around and disappears down the hill. She is upset, Tom thinks. Like him, she has seen that it is a bad nest. The mud walls crumbling around her. The farms below also bad nests. They have given them land and that is not nothing. But these tiny squares of earth do not contain appeasement, they contain nothing but dirt. Even Tom can see this.

Tom and Jose stand alone on the slope. After a long silence Tom says to Jose they may as well finish the tour. Now that they are here. It being such a nice spring day. He does not know what else to do. Jose nods and they turn their horses back down the hill to the flat land below. Jose leads him around the pasture, in a long and sloping square. Tom asks him what is theirs and Jose tells him that it is this square and what he has already seen, something like one thousand acres. What good will that do me, asks Tom. I don't know but it's yours, says Jose.

Tom points to the land surrounding their square.

"They haven't allocated our land."

"Not yet."

"When will they do it?"

"Soon, I think."

"And what were we doing with it?"

"Nothing."

Tom nods. That cannot strictly speaking be true and yet he understands what Jose means. The old man left things fallow more often than not, his own son included. Until the time came to harvest at will. Tom looked down across the valley. At the land, which has been the only frame for his vision. He thought: the old man had liked a picture. He had liked a vista. An empty legacy, a stupid one, now that time had come to an end.

It will not be recovered. Soon these fields would also be covered in fence and barbed wire. Like a million cages set upon their land. They would be surrounded and there would be nothing to be done about it. Tom draws his breath in through his nose.

"Is it all like this?"

Jose nods.

"Everywhere?"

He shrugs. They turn and ride back to the house.

When they arrive, the girl is nowhere to be seen. She has vanished. Her bags have been packed and the drawers of the dresser in her room are empty. Tom stands in the stable and wipes the horses down. The mare had not been untacked. They had found her standing in the stable yard, the reins hastily thrown over a post. Tom unbuckles the harness and the horse exhales in relief. He rubs her down and the muzzle is soft as felt.

9

The house sits empty without the girl. Meanwhile the old man is much worse. He has gone into free fall. It is official. There is a measurable difference each day. Every change is a bad one. His limbs are swollen with the sickness. His skin is slick and glossy and his eyes have grown cloudy—his eyes are so cloudy it is impossible to believe they contain vision.

He cannot walk. He cannot sit up. Now he can only lie in bed and stare at the ceiling and call for more morphine. He says that he cannot breathe, I am having difficulty breathing. He tries to describe it to them. It is like someone is stealing my air. Like someone—he claws at his chest and throat. Like this. It is like this. He asks for more morphine.

Tom brings him the bottle. The old man's eyes glitter as he looks at it. His eyes do not move as he watches Tom tap out one, two pills and then set the bottle down.

The old man grabs Tom's arm. He lifts three fingers.

"Two."

The old man shakes his head. He lifts three fingers again.

"I can only give you two."

The old man shuts his eyes and shakes his head. His voice spent by frustration. Tom reaches for the glass of water.

"Open."

The old man nods and opens his mouth and sticks his tongue out. Lips quivering. Tongue dry as dust. Tom drops the pills onto his tongue and raises the glass to his mouth. Gently he presses the old man's jaw shut. He watches him swallow and close his eyes. His face becomes calm.

"Sleep. Until the medicine takes effect."

The old man nods. He is covered to the neck and only his head protrudes above the edge of the quilt. Tom raises his hand to check his temperature. He stands up, bottle and glass in hand. His father does not open his eyes again.

Tom goes into the kitchen. Celeste takes the glass from his hand. She doesn't look at him as she returns to the stove.

"I will take the meal in to him."

He nods. His father no longer cares who serves him. He is not able to see much beyond the pain. It has got to that point. And Tom no longer cares to take the meal in himself. He is happy for Celeste to do this. She stirs a pot vigorously then sets down the spoon.

"He is not well."

"We are running out of morphine."

"This morning, when I went into his room—"

"There is enough for another week. If we do not up the dosage, and we may need to. The medicine does not last as long as it did even a couple days ago."

"—he was calling out."

"It was six hours and now it is only four. Tomorrow it will be only three."

"And he was in distress. He had fouled himself."

"Celeste, listen—"

"The shit was everywhere. All over the sheets. Some of it dripping onto the floor. He had shat right through his pajamas. He was crying and crying and I do not know how long he had been lying there like this, in his own shit and nobody listening. Nobody knowing."

Tom falls silent. He sits down. He cannot look at Celeste. She is crying. A tear, another, one by one. Falling into the soup.

"The smell was terrible. I opened the door and I couldn't breathe. I don't know how he lay there all that time. And the shit—the shit was black as tar. Sticky like pitch."

Tom does not want to hear this. He is stumbling, his legs are buckling, beneath the weight of the situation. The girl has gone. The old man sits in a pile of his own shit. And there is the rebellion. Will it come to them? Despite himself, he asks the question. It is impossible. Surely it is impossible. He looks at Celeste. He cannot discuss the matter with her. She has her own emotions to tend to, it is better that they keep to themselves.

He rises to his feet and asks her to look after the old man's cleanliness. To make certain that he has not soiled himself. He is not entirely himself anymore, he says to her. He says this to her and also to himself. The old man is himself and he is also something very, very different.

Tom goes outside and sits down on the stoop. His day is filled with tasks. He feeds the old man. He checks his temperature. He changes the bed sheets. He counts the hours between pills. The days will disappear in the counting—all his time will go and then the old man will be dead and Tom will not even know where to begin. He knows only this: that when the old man dies, there will be no place for him to put all his feeling.

He is aware of a deep and growing numbness, which is spreading through his body. He can no longer think, his brain sits beneath a heavy mass of unexplored emotion. While the numbness inches across his body. Soon he will not be able to move, he thinks. Soon it will be just like he has been paralyzed, from the waist down, from the neck down, from the top of his head down to the floor.

Yes, he is tired, it is like they warned him. Tom tries to imagine the farm with the old man dead, he tries to imagine what that will mean. But without the girl and the inheritance he has no way of understanding the old man's death. Without the girl there is nothing but the old man lying in the bed, and the old man stops all acts of imagination. He freezes the son in the present tense. Although he himself continues to die, and soon will be gone.

Tom gets up from the stoop. He goes back into the house and to the old man's room. He hopes he will be asleep. The old man asleep and dying is easier than the old man awake and dying. The old man awake is becoming more than Tom can handle. Every interaction is increasingly strange. Each interaction is becoming a horror show.

He is not asleep. He is awake and staring at the ceiling and smiling. His eyes crawling across the wall. His hands petting and patting the covers. He looks at Tom when he comes in. It takes a moment. He motions for him to sit down.

Cautiously, Tom sits down. The old man motions for him to come closer. Which Tom does, a little. The old man motions for him to come closer still. Tom hesitates and then moves forward until he can smell the sour odor rising from the old man's mouth. The residue of shit from the floorboards. Something new, something he has not noticed before—a sweet smell, the sweet smell of the sickness, like confectionery, seeping out of the old man's skin. He sniffs and pushes his nose closer while his father's eyes roam the ceiling and down the wall.

"Did she go?"

He jolts back. The girl, who has been gone a week if not longer. The old man leers at him conspiratorially. As if to say, You and I both know what I am talking about. And Tom does in fact know. But he does not know what the old man means by the leer and the wink.

"Do you mean Carine?"

"*Tccch.*"

That's all his father says. His fingers back to patting the cover in place. His eyes back to roaming the ceiling. He is smiling. Wistfully, like he is listening to nostalgic music in his head. Tom has never seen his father like this. The old man does not smile. Not like this and not wistfully. Tom shakes his head.

"She is gone."

He hopes the fact of the girl's departure will bring his father back. But his father is a million miles away. He waves his hands in the air like he is conducting an orchestra. Then he folds his hands together and rests them on the quilt. He closes his eyes. He is still smirking.

Tom realizes that if he had a different relationship with his father, if he loved him in a way he understood, in a way that he knew to be normal, if the numbness had not overtaken his body—then he would have found this tragic. He would have been weeping into his cup of tea the way Celeste weeps into her pot of soup. But he is not. He does not have access to those tears.

Tom stands up. The old man is asleep and there is no point in his staying. He exits the room and returns to the kitchen. Left alone, the old man opens his eyes and goes back to crawling the walls with his vision.

Tom sits down at the kitchen table. His father's eyes on the bottle. The gleam against the cloudy pupils. His thoughts return to the problem of the medicine. The old man is lusting after the pills the way he once lusted after women. And he is a man whose needs must be satisfied. He will need more pills. He will need them very soon. Tom has a headache. He tries to think through the throbbing. He thinks the nearest doctor is in Herbertville, sixty kilometers away.

He thinks but is not sure. He has never been to Herbertville. He believes it is a day's journey. He has no idea how to organize such a journey. On a horse? In the car? Alone or with help? (Not alone. He will not do such a thing alone.) He tries to imagine himself walking the streets of Herbertville. He tries to imagine how he will explain it to the doctor. Pain management, he thinks they call it. After a certain point you have to concentrate on pain management.

He will need money for the doctor. And he will need a horse. The car is useless, the car is barely running, and then there is the fact that he does not know how to drive. Tom does not know if going to Herbertville is a good idea but he understands that he is a man without choice. People shoot cattle in the head when they are too far gone for saving. The old man is too far gone for saving but shooting him in the head is not an option as far as Tom can tell.

No—the gun being out of the picture, Tom will go find a doctor, who will give him more pills and tell him about the pain management. He will need to get Jose to travel with him. Jose is a good horseman. He has traveled the roads and knows the area well. And Jose is good with people. Tom is not good with people. He does not do well with strangers, not even with people he knows. But Jose—yes, Jose is different.

With this in mind Tom goes to find him. He walks the road leading to the stables. This road is generally deserted and runs clear and unimpeded across the land. He can therefore see the men in the distance. He counts four or possibly five. They come down the road, down from the farm, riding bicycles. They have tied plastic bags to the backs of the seats and there are plastic bags hanging and swinging from the handlebars.

Mystified, Tom stops and watches the men approach. His men, they are his natives. The sound of wheels whirring fast as the bags rock and jolt and are covered in dust. The men wear bandannas across their faces and dark glasses to protect their eyes. They have large rucksacks strapped to their backs and humpbacked they roll forward, they occupy the road, gaining speed as they move.

Two-wheeled as they are, they catapult toward him. Tom leaps to the side of the road. They come within a single foot of him but swarm past without stopping—they act as if they do not see him, their eyes invisible behind the sunglasses and road goggles. They pedal furiously and the dust rises ten feet into the air as they go.

Within seconds they are gone. Tom stares after them as they disappear down the road. They move past the gate and exit the farm. He stares at the empty road. It is silent. The stables are quiet. He listens to insect sounds and watches the dust cloud settle to the ground. He stares at the earth and is baffled.

He turns and then sees another group of men. A sea of them coming down the road on bicycles and motorcycles, these men carrying their wives and children. The men ignore him but some of the women and children, some nod or wave as they pass. None of them slow. None stop to explain. They churn more dust instead, they toss the dirt back up into the air.

They are fleeing. The last of the farmhands are leaving. They are abandoning the estate. This time Tom runs after them. He shouts into their cloud of dust.

"Where are you going? What are you doing?"

Still they do not stop and so he runs faster, waving his arms.

"What has happened? Why are you leaving?"

He is talking to a mountain of dust. They are meters away, they are half the distance to the gate, they have disappeared down the road. He stares after them. He turns and looks back at the farm. It is silent again. He watches as the road dust settles. He looks for the men, he tries to spot them in the distance, but they have disappeared and the landscape is still.

He hears a whirring sound behind him. A young boy comes cycling down the road after the pack. Tom races into the road and flings his arms out.

"Stop! Stop!"

The boy swerves and tumbles off his bicycle. He scrambles to his feet, hopping. There is a cut across his knee. Tom looks at the boy's face. He is not certain that he has seen him before. He does not know his name.

"Where are you going?"

The boy shakes his head and rights the bicycle.

"Tell me where you are going!"

"It is not safe here."

Tom laughs.

"What are you talking about?"

"The rebellion is coming. The men who go to the forest—they are coming."

Tom grabs the boy by the shoulders.

"You are just a little boy. You do not know what you are talking about."

The boy shakes himself free.

"Mister, I know what I am talking about."

He gets back on the bicycle.

"I have to go. They will not wait for me."

"Who will not wait? Where are you going?"

The boy shakes his head and calls out as he pedals away.

"I know what I am talking about! You will see!"

Tom watches him cycle down the road and then disappear. The farm is now completely silent. He whirls around and runs to the house. He finds Jose by the stables. He is smoking a cigarette. Tom stops in front of him, gasping for breath.

"What is it? Why have they gone?"

Jose looks at him. In the silence, Tom becomes increasingly aware of Jose's contempt. Which for the first time he displays to Tom without mitigation. He takes his time before replying.

"They have gone."

"Yes, but where?"

Tom is still trying to recover his breath. Jose stubs out his cigarette on the ground and then carefully retrieves the butt. He holds it in his fingers.

"They are afraid."

"I don't understand."

"I know."

He looks at Tom.

"I hope they will not come so far as the valley. But you should be prepared."

"Prepared—for what?"

"There has been killing everywhere. Do you not listen to the radio? It started in the north and it has spread. For the past month they have been moving toward the south."

Jose pauses. He shrugs.

"Now they have reached the south. The rebellion is here."

Tom stares at the dirt and the dust. He has never listened to the radio, he is not interested by it. He does not even read the paper. He licks at his mouth, nervous.

"Violence about what? We gave them the land. They are taking it. We saw, just the other day—"

Tom is like a blind man. He does not see what is about to hit him in the face and knock him down. It has been shown to him but he has been looking the other way. Jose is not inclined to explain, perhaps believing the task to be insurmountable. He shrugs again.

"Yes."

"One acre a man. Isn't that enough? We are all the same now."

"You have one thousand acres. You are a single man."

"That is different."

"Yes."

"I will give them more land. If more land is what they want."

"It is too late."

Tom needs to gather his thoughts. He takes out a pack of cigarettes. He offers the pack to Jose.

"We need to go to Herbertville."

Jose shakes his head.

"Too dangerous."

"He needs more medicine."

"It is too dangerous."

"He will die if we do not go."

"You should not be here. Do you understand?"

Tom shakes his head. The old man will die either way. The old man is bound to death. But either he will die and that will be that, or the work of dying itself will kill him. The logic is impenetrable but solid as rock in Tom's head. He reaches up and seizes Jose by the shoulder.

"He will die. I need you to go with me."

Jose shakes his head. Tom drops his hands. Jose fishes in his pocket for a lighter and goes back to smoking.

"I will give you something. If you go."

"What can you give me?"

"Money. There is still some money."

"How much?"

"Two hundred dollars."

Jose puffs at his cigarette. For the first time it occurs to Tom: he tells Tom to go, but why does he stay when the others have gone? It cannot be loyalty. Tom does not believe in Jose's loyalty. He stays, Tom thinks, out of force of habit. He is too used to them. Too used to the whites. Celeste is the same way. They cannot break the habit in the way of the others. There are too many links, of which they are barely aware. Tom waits for Jose to speak.

"I will need to see the money first."

"Of course."

"And we go together."

"Yes. How long will it take?"

"Half a day by the back roads. Maybe a little longer."

"If we leave in the night, can we be back in one day?"

"Possibly."

Tom nods. He needs to sit down. He is feeling faint. His breath is coming short and sweat is breaking out across his forehead. He sits down on the ground, in the dirt, chest heaving. Jose looks down at him.

"What are you doing?"

He waves him off. He sits cross-legged and wheezes. He keeps his head tipped down into his chest. He waits for his breath to slow.

"Are you well enough to travel?"

Tom swallows and looks up at Jose.

"I am fine. We can leave tomorrow."

Jose puts his hands into his pockets. He does not offer Tom his hand. He does not help him to his feet. He looks down at him. Tom sits in the dirt and watches Jose, who frowns.

"Okay."

Slowly, Tom gets to his feet. He reaches out to shake Jose's hand. Jose hesitates and then takes Tom's hand. They are both confused by the gesture. Now Tom dreads the journey ahead. What is he doing? Perhaps they are both fools. After all, they are the only ones left. He should have gone long ago. But he did not and instead is still stuck on the land, it is him and the dying man, here on the farm.

10

They leave at three in the morning. It is black dark outside. Tom does not like the dark—he is the kind of man who sleeps with a sliver of light. He is the kind of man who likes a candle by his bed. He is nervous and rides his horse poorly. Lucky for him the horse is placid and used to his nervousness. The horse plods ahead and stays the course despite the darkness.

Jose rides ahead and is inscrutable. This is the word Tom uses in his head. The word they all use and have used, to describe the natives. It is not accurate, the natives being as readable as any of the white settlers, if the white settlers took the time to do the reading. However, they do not and have not. Nonetheless, as far as Tom can tell he is as interested in completing the journey as Tom and that is a source of some reassurance.

According to Jose, they can take the main road for the first half of the journey. The rebellion has not yet come this far south. Jose knows the movements of the rebellion in uncanny detail. Having never spoken of it before, the rebellion is now all Jose speaks of. The rebellion is here or it is there. The rebellion is moving toward them. It is moving away. The rebellion is growing in speed and strength.

This new idea of the rebellion is making Tom unhinged. He rides the horse and his entrails thrash inside him. He does not even know what the rebellion means. And yet his vocabulary expands. There are new words and new ideas. The Oath Takers. The men who've gone to the forest. The expansion is no good thing for Tom. He lives in a permanent state of contraction and the stretching is like to break him.

He asks questions. In the dark he babbles out of nervousness.

"And what is their oath?"

"The oath is for land and freedom."

"But we have given them land and they have their freedom."

"Maybe it is not enough."

"Who says they are not free? They are free."

"We should not talk. We must be silent."

Jose is also tense. All the others have left. The punishment for collusion is worse than death. And yet he stays! When logic dictated his departure long ago. He has been hedging his bets, he tells himself he is only hedging his bets. But his position will not be sustainable for long. Soon he will need to make a decision.

Therefore he remains silent as they ride. The roads are empty and dark. There are small herds of sheep and cattle but no humans to speak of. After two hours the road runs up the hills and directly through the territory of the new farms. Loops of barbed wire hang from sticks and in some cases there are wire fences. Most farms have nothing more than a single shack. Not large enough for a family, barely large enough for a couple of tools and a plow. The farms are all fence and barbed wire.

None of the land looks like it is being used. It looks like acres of divided dirt fields. They are not large enough to grow anything. A vegetable garden. Some wheat or corn.

The new farms are by and large useless. Tom sees that. He is not surprised that the farms are deserted. Jose says to him that they should go. They should keep away from the new farms and villages. He says they are not deserted, far from it. Tom shakes his head. The new farms are everywhere. They are unavoidable. Look, he says. Look how they are eating up the land.

But Jose is uneasy. He says to him that they must go. Now. They leave the main road and go up the hills. They are no-where close to Herbertville, they are nowhere near half done with their journey, and already they have taken to the back roads. These roads are curving and winding and indirect. Tom does not like the logic of the back roads. After an hour of riding in what feels like circles, Tom tells Jose they should return to the main road. He says to him that they are losing time. It is past dawn. It is nearly morning.

We are not so far, Jose says. We are making good time—

He is cut off by the sound of gunfire. Both men jump. A long silence and then a long round of shots. The sound of voices shouting. They dismount and pull their horses into shadow. Jose motions to Tom, he puts a finger to his lips. Tom nods, teeth chattering. He whispers to himself, he says, perhaps it is a hunt, yes, maybe that is what it is. That would explain it. They are hunting impala. They are hunting wild boar. Jose glares at him and motions again for him to be silent. He peers through the bushes.

The next round of gunfire is all around them. It is in every direction. Tom covers his ears. He buries his head and closes his eyes. The reins slip through his fingers—in an instant, the horse has bolted and is gone. He hears men shouting and he cowers down closer to the ground. He wishes to disappear, for the ground to swallow him whole—he should never have left the farm.

The voices come closer—they are on this road, this dirt road, they are right there, they should have stuck to the main road, another mistake—and then there is a long silence and he is forced from terror to open his eyes. Jose is nowhere in sight. Both horses have disappeared. It is only him, what they call Lizard Boy, crouching in the dirt and dust. He stands. The sun is high in the sky. He squints and raises an arm to block the sun.

"Don't move."

He freezes in the middle of the road.

"Turn. Slowly."

He shuffles his feet in the dirt. A young man dressed in full army uniform stands behind him carrying an AK-47. Tom is cautious but relieved. This makes sense. The Government will have sent soldiers to the valley, having heard of the rebellion's course. They will have sent troops to protect the citizens of the country.

"Raise your hands."

Cautiously, he raises his hands. He wishes the young man would not point the machine gun at his chest—it is hardly necessary, look, he is white, clearly he is not an Oath Taker! But the young man does not lower the rifle. Instead he steps closer until the barrel of the gun is pressing into Tom's sternum and then he stops. He is not even a man. He is just a boy. Tom's heart thumps against the gun's metal barrel.

The boy soldier calls out.

"Over here!"

He is joined by an older soldier. This solder has a shotgun strapped to his leg and his uniform is not as clean as the boy's—there are rips and tear and stains and the sleeves appear to have fallen off altogether. Perhaps he has been fighting the rebellion for some time now, since it started up north. He wears a colonel's stripes and medals. His green trousers are tucked into his boots and the boots are covered in dirt and grime. He comes to Tom and the boy.

"Who is this?"

"I found him here, crouching by the side of the road."

"Where?"

"Here. Here."

The boy soldier jerks the rifle to the ground. His eyes remain on Tom.

"Is he armed?"

"No."

The older soldier looks at Tom.

"What are you doing here?"

"I came to get medicine for my father."

"What is wrong with him?"

"He is dying."

"You are all dying."

Tom nods. He is becoming afraid again. He would like to go. These people are frightening to him. Their faces are crossed with scars and he sees now that they are splattered with new blood. The boy soldier has a machete slung into his trousers. Tom does not know if this is right or wrong. There are things, definitely there are things about these men that are not right. They seem very close to deranged. They have spent too long in the forest and lost their minds.

"Soon you will be gone. This country is no longer safe for white men."

"Yes. We will be leaving."

"And going where?"

"Home."

The older soldier laughs.

"Yes. That is the right answer. I see that you are learning."

He smiles and scratches his chin. He looks up at the sun lazily.

"Tell me. Have you heard of the birds called Rheas?"

Tom shakes his head, mute with fear. The soldier smiles.

"No? They are big birds—too big to fly. They gather on the ground with nothing to do. Imagine. So many birds, gathered on the ground and none of them able to fly away. There is not enough land for so many birds."

Comically, he lifts an eyebrow.

"They must find a way to occupy themselves. They must find a way to keep themselves busy. A game."

He pauses. He wags a finger at Tom and lowers his voice confidentially.

"This is a game the male birds play. They clear a large space and then two male birds lock necks. They spin in a circle with their necks locked. They spin faster and faster until one of the birds becomes dizzy and lets go. The dizzy bird is the loser. The one that lets go first. That is how they make the time pass."

He looks at Tom.

"Have you heard this story before?"

This time Tom nods.

"It is a good story, no? These birds are as big as men. As big as human beings."

He sighs. He looks up at the sun again.

"Time to go."

He signals to the boy and then turns and heads down the path. The boy soldier looks after him.

"What do I do with him?"

"Leave him. He is harmless."

The older soldier disappears down the road. The boy soldier turns to Tom. His gun still leveled at his chest. He keeps the gun trained on him and then abruptly lowers it. He grimaces.

"You are a lucky guy."

He turns and jogs down the road after the older soldier. They disappear into the bush.

For a long time Tom stands frozen in the middle of the road. Eventually he lowers his hands. They have been up, held up in the air all this time. Now he lowers them and they are sore with the effort. He hears—birds, trees, stupid and anonymous sounds. He is alone. He is safe and still alive. He knows he has been lucky, he does not need the boy soldier to tell him this. The blood—his life, now saved, of which he is newly aware—pounds through his head.

In the distance he hears a round of gunfire. Followed by shouts. Quickly, he crouches down in the middle of the road, he hides behind a bush. The shouts gather into a song. He strains to hear the words.

The men who go to the forest
The men who drink the oath
We will fight
Until we take back the land
Down to the last man
Down to the last shout
Better to die standing
Than on your knees
Better to die free
Than a slave

He covers his ears with his hands in horror and waits for the voices to fade as the men pull into the distance. When he can no longer hear the voices he stands. He is trembling all over. He ducks into the bush and runs as fast as he can. He is getting lost—he is already lost. He does not know where he is going apart from away.

Tom runs as fast as Tom can run. He runs but it turns out there is nowhere to go. He runs and finds himself down on the main road. The moment he sees the expanse of paved surface he panics and ducks back into the bush. He crouches in the dirt and listens for the all clear of silence. There are smells in the air—smoke and blood, he can smell both smoke and blood.

His thoughts are disordered. He needs to get a horse. He must find Jose. He must find a way to get home, he must warn his father of the soldiers. I am looking for help. He says this to himself. I am looking for help. He stands up and steps into the road. Up ahead he sees a house in flames. It burns close to the ground and is half in ember.

He starts walking in the direction of the burning house, not knowing where else to go. He has lost his shoes—how? He cannot tell how long his feet have been bare—and the soil is hot from sun and flame. His feet and legs have been cut from thorns and bramble. He stumbles as he walks and then he is grabbed, seized, by both arms and pulled to the ground. He chokes as the air is pushed out of his lungs and coughs as the dust flies up into his face.

Jose clamps his hand over his mouth and motions for him to be silent. Tom pries his hand off.

"Where have you been?"

"Quiet."

Tom lowers his voice to a whisper.

"Where have you been?"

"Are you okay?"

"Those soldiers—there was something wrong with them."

"Those were no soldiers. You should be dead."

"Who were they?"

"Oath Takers."

"They were in uniform."

"They steal uniforms off the dead. They have seized this entire area."

"But—how?"

Jose motions for them to get off the road. They crouch—like animals, like less than animals—in the dirt and bush. From this position, close to the ground, they see a group of men on the road. A handful carry AK-47s and there are machetes as well. They do not appear to be in any hurry, they move at a leisurely pace. They fire their guns—sometimes into the air, sometimes at a target up ahead on the road, not visible to either Tom or Jose.

"They are on the move. The men who questioned you— which way did they go?"

Tom indicates the road east. These men also go east. They pass and Tom and Jose lie still, flat on the ground, underneath the bush. They are followed by more and then more men. There are not that many, they are maybe two or three dozen. But they fill the road, they are grabbing hold of it as they go. No wonder—it occurs to Tom, Tom thinks to himself, they will take this country. They will take it. If thirty men can do this then with three hundred, with three thousand, the country will be theirs.

They believe it belongs to them, or they do not care and will take it anyway, in any case it will be theirs, he can see it. Things are splintering around him, Tom can feel the foundation crack. It will never be put together again. It is not going to be restored. He gasps for breath. It is like he is growing transparent, like he himself is now becoming invisible, as in front of him the terrain is hacked to machete slices.

It is no wonder they do not see him. The Oath Takers patrol the road. Everything around them falls silent. Even the animals and the animal noises. The rebel soldiers walk with swagger and exaggerated grimness. Their limbs are loose and they pull faces and shout to fill out the silence. We are performing a duty. We are doing what needs to be done for the country. Behind them is a trail of justified blood and they are carrying, they are dragging, the trail forward.

Tom and Jose crouch in the shadow of the trees and wait for the men to go. They are not very many but they come in small clusters, it takes a long time for them to go. Even when they are gone Tom is afraid to move. After a little while, Jose swallows.

"They are gone."

Tom nods. He no longer remembers what they have come here to do. It seems a long time ago, it seems far away. He crouches beside Jose, trembling. His legs have the cramp and he cannot move them. Jose turns to him.

"Let's go."

"We should wait a little longer."

"No. Let's go. Now."

He steps out into the road and Tom has no choice but to follow. He scrambles after Jose.

"Where are you going?"

Jose stops.

"I am going in the opposite direction from the rebels. That is where I am going."

He turns and continues down the road in the direction of the village. Tom scrambles to catch up. Black smoke rises up from the soil and into the air. Up ahead, the rebels have torched the shacks and houses. They have torched anything that will burn. The side of the road is lined with giant heaps of hot ash and ember. Tom and Jose walk along the ash heaps and the air is full of smoke and the smell of blood and charring.

They should go, Tom says. He wants to go, he does not understand what they are doing. His voice rising to a screech. Tom has been unfastened by panic. He only wants to go, now. But Jose is not listening. Jose is ignoring Tom. He steps from the road and begins looking through the rubble. He lifts pieces of charred wood, blackened metal and finds a body. The head has been hacked off with a machete. Jose ignores the black stump of bone and vein and carefully opens the pockets. He pulls out a gold chain. A couple of bills. He takes these and pushes the body away.

"Jose! Jose!"

There is a warmth spreading through the seat of his trousers and down to the ground. A puddle of hot piss growing in the dirt. Tom cries and whimpers and continues to piss himself. The relief and hot warmth being a comfort while Jose moves further down the road, looking for bodies, poking through the ash. He finds things and they make their way into his pockets. He looks back at Tom.

"Come."

Reluctantly, Tom follows him, soaked in piss, his bare feet completely wet. Jose strides ahead, having picked up a rifle. Tom does not know when Jose found the gun. Now he carries it over his shoulder like he has always carried a rifle over his shoulder. Tom can smell the acidic register of his own clothes, soaked as they are in urine. In front is more smoke and more bodies. A chicken wailing in distress.

They enter the village. An army jeep has been overturned in the middle of the road. It lies on its side like a dead animal. The glass has been shattered and the driver hangs limp from the half open door. He has been shot in the head and his mouth is wrenched open in protest and his palms are spread into the dust.

Around the jeep are dead soldiers—real Government soldiers this time. They are sprawled across the road like they have been flung there by way of explosion. Their torsos are slashed and entrails spill into the dusty road, viscera sit in the dirt. The rebels have stripped the soldiers of their jackets and boots. Their feet are coated in a layer of fine dust. They have also taken all the guns.

By the side of the road bodies hang from trees like spectators made to watch against their will, not finding the entertainment to their liking. Their trousers are twisted around their ankles and their faces are petrified. Their mouths stuffed with their own testicles, they are slack jawed with shock and surprise. Their penises lie shriveled and scattered in the dirt beneath their feet. Tom vomits and then wipes his face with his shirt. The smell is terrible.

It is terrible and it is everywhere. There are bodies in the road and in the trees and there are children as well as women and men. Women and men as well as soldiers. The killing has been expert and senseless. Up ahead a tree is also burning. The fire spreads from branch to branch. It jumps from limb to limb. The whole thing will burn down, thinks Tom. The entire forest will be destroyed.

"Tom!"

He turns. Jose stands by the army truck, he is attempting to prize a canvas case from the collapsed trunk of the vehicle. He motions to Tom.

"Here. Help me."

The case is enveloped in warped steel and rubber. They try to bend the metal with their bare hands. Jose steps back. He yanks an abandoned machete from a dead man's torso. He returns to the jeep and hacks into the metal until the case is free. He snaps it open. It is full of syringes and vials and pills. He examines the labels and then tosses the case to Tom.

"What is it?"

"There is some morphine. Take it."

Tom takes the case.

"What now?"

"We need to find horses."

"Where?"

He shrugs. He turns and goes deeper into the village. Tom thinks about not following. He thinks about waiting here by the jeep. Soon Jose disappears and Tom is left alone. He looks—in every direction is a dead body, a rotting body, a burnt corpse. He hurries after Jose and hears a crack like loud thunder. The burning tree has fallen into the road and is blocking it. Jose looks at Tom.

"Take off your jacket and cover your face."

"Let's go back. Jose, let's go back."

"We need horses. There will be horses somewhere in the village."

He wraps his head in his own jacket and bolts forward, the rifle cradled in his arms. He leaps over the burning rubble. Tom stares after him. He leaps and hops and jumps and then stops. Only his feet and head are visible through the smoke. He motions for Tom to follow, a movement Tom sees dimly through the smoke and debris. Tom shakes his head. Jose pulls the jacket off and turns to go. Left with no choice, Tom removes his jacket and plunges down the road.

At the other end, Jose pulls him out and thumps him on the back. One. Two. Three. Tom gulps fresh air and is better. He wipes the soot from his face and eyes and can see. Ahead on the road are more bodies, more overturned army vehicles. Jose points.

"Look. There are horses."

And in fact there are horses. There are three, there are four, standing by the side of the road. Jose walks forward with his hands by his side. He moves like the old man, Tom suddenly realizes. He has become exactly like him. Tom sees, in a flash of understanding, that this is also part of the new order. That Jose should take the place of the old man. Tom watches as Jose slides to the horses, he holds his palm out, they approach, he grips their manes and then they are no longer free.

The horses' owners are more than likely dead, somewhere ahead or behind them on the road. Jose tells Tom to mount the calmest and the broadest horse. He has found some rope, he uses it to lead the other two horses, two horses in addition to the two they ride, four horses altogether, what will he do with four horses? The horses are terrified by the chaos and are reassured by being led. They are comforted by the human weight astride their backs.

Jose leads the two spare horses and also Tom and his horse and together they make their way down the road, out of the village. The horses jumping over the bodies in the road. Where are we going? Tom asks. We will circle around, says Jose, we will find our way back to the farm. You have the morphine, he says. You have the case? Yes, Tom says. I have the case. So you see, we found what we were looking for in the end. Yes, Tom says. Yes.

They are ten minutes outside the village before the smell of burning flesh and blood is gone. The rebels must have come this way, says Jose. But there is no sign of it. They pass a large farm with a gate and emblem. Jose stops.

"I know this farm."

Tom nods.

"It belongs to the Wallaces."

Tom nods again. There is a large stone house, visible from the gate. Jose looks up at the house. Then he quickly dismounts and ties the horses to the gate.

"What are you doing?"

"I am getting more morphine."

"We have morphine. I have it right here."

"That will only last a few days. The Wallaces are addicts."

Tom does not know how Jose knows the Wallaces are addicts, how he knows this and so many other things. He watches Jose disappear down the path. He has no choice but to tie his own horse and follow him. The house windows are broken and the door is charred black. Jose kicks the door open. He enters ahead of Tom and he holds the AK-47 at the level of his waist. He could be an Oath Taker for all Tom knows. Nothing would surprise me now. Everything is surprising me now. It is one or the other, he is not sure.

The house is empty and it is silent, in a bad way. There are pieces of furniture overturned and there are bullet holes in the wall and splashes of blood on the floor, on the wall, on the overturned furniture. Jose stops and listens but the house is silent. He nods and goes to the dresser. He opens drawers, he looks for bottles and syringes. In the process he pockets things—jewels, coins, packets of bills and bonds—that the rebels have missed or not looked for at all.

Tom goes into the sitting room and finds Mrs. Wallace. Who has been slashed in the throat and torso. She sits on the sofa secreting a stream of blood. The cushions are stained and there are splatters of blood on the walls and on the floor. Mrs. Wallace stares up at the ceiling. Her expression is one of shock and disapproval. The family hounds lie on the floor around her, shot in the head and chest, tongues draped from their open jaws.

Tom stares at Mrs. Wallace. He has not seen her since the girl first came to the farm. When all the trouble began, a long time ago. Now Mrs. Wallace sits frozen in this well-furnished room. There are pillows and throws on the chairs, not all of which are ruined by blood. There are brass lamps and paintings on the wall. A trio of flies buzzes around Mrs. Wallace's head. One and then another lands on her open eye. Which is turning to jelly, her eyes are decaying quickly in the heat. Soon they will slide out of their sockets like liquid gel.

Slowly, Tom backs away. Then he turns and runs out of the room. He is running past the marble heads and silver cigar boxes, past the walnut credenza and the cupboards, the mahogany cupboards that line the room. He is knocking over chairs and occasional tables in his haste to get out of the room. When one of the cupboard doors swings open and a foot, a leg, the girl steps out of the furniture. Tom comes to a halt.

Of course she would have come here. Of course they would have taken her in. These are times of trouble but they are family. The girl is family. Even in her current state. Tom can understand. But it is still a shock to see the girl and her belly, climbing out of the cupboard, coughing to clear the dust

that has gathered in her throat over the hours—how many?—
she has spent hidden, cramped inside the cupboard.

Tom stares at her. He opens his mouth.

"Mrs. Wallace—"

"I don't want to look."

He nods. Jose enters the room and looks at both of them. He
does not seem surprised to see Carine. Yes—Jose has become
like the old man. Who is also seldom very surprised. Briefly,
Jose looks across the room at Mrs. Wallace. Then he looks at
the girl.

"So you came here."

"Yes."

"How did you survive? Where did you hide?"

"I hid in the cupboard. I was sitting with Martha when they
arrived. There wasn't time to hide anyplace else."

"And Mrs. Wallace?"

"She did not move quickly enough."

"Unfortunate for her."

The girl shrugs. Jose looks away.

"Where is Mr. Wallace?"

"They shot him outside."

Jose nods. He is carrying a leather satchel and it is full to
bursting with pills and vials and gold and silver objects. He
looks at the girl.

"Where is the safe?"

She shakes her head.

"I don't know."

"We will need money."

"I know."

"Then where is the safe?"

"Her jewels are upstairs in her dressing room."

They leave Mrs. Wallace on the sofa and follow the girl up the stairs. She stops by a window on the second floor and points out the window.

"Look. There is Robert."

A man lies facedown in a ditch. His back is riddled with bullets. Jose looks out the window, then continues down the hall. The girl looks out the window a little longer, then quickly turns away. They reach the dressing room. Inside there are silk gowns and feathers and flowers. The faint smell of perfume. Through an open door, the bathroom is visible. The tub sits full of lukewarm water.

Jose walks to the vanity table. He sets the rifle on the gilt and glass surface. He picks up and pries open a jewel box and begins lifting out necklaces and bracelets. He pauses and looks up at the girl.

"You should wash the soot off."

She nods and goes into the bathroom, where she sponges her face and arms and legs with the water in the bath. Jose empties two boxes full of diamonds and sapphires and pearls into his satchel. He drops in ebony hairbrushes and mother of pearl hair clips. He finds, at the bottom of the stocking drawer, a wad of bills tied with a piece of string.

The girl appears, rubbing her hair with a towel. She has changed into a dress and sweater, she wears boots and carries a bag. Jose looks up.

"We should go."

She nods. Jose briefly surveys the room. Then he picks up the satchel and rifle. They go downstairs in a line, Jose and then Carine and then Tom. When they reach the front entrance, Jose looks at the girl. He grips the gun in his arms and nods to her.

"You aren't staying."

"Here? No."

"Then you may as well come."

"Yes," she says. "Yes. I may as well come."

11

The horses are still tied to the Wallaces' gate. Tom helps the girl mount and then he and Jose mount their rides. Jose leading the fourth horse. The girl holds out her hand.

"Give me a gun."

Jose looks at her. She keeps her hand out and stares back at him.

"I mean it."

He reaches into the back of his trousers and pulls out a pistol, which he hands to her. The AK-47 remains on his lap. The girl's hands tremble a little. She checks the magazine for bullets and thumbs the safety, then tucks the pistol into her boot. She nods to Jose. He hesitates, then brings out another pistol and hands it to Tom.

"Here."

Tom takes the gun. There is powder at the barrel. He grips the gun and the reins and nods to both of them. The weight of the gun in his fingers.

"Let's go."

They go back through the village. In order to return to the farm they must retrace their steps. It is nearly noon. The sun is directly overhead. The bodies are melting in the sun. Already there are flies gathering in the holes and crevices of the corpses. The smell is awful. The horses are calm, preferring the smell of rot to the smell of blood, but to the humans, the smell is unbearable.

Jose looks back at them.

"Cover your nose and mouth."

The girl's body loses balance and momentarily she sways in the saddle. Her belly plunging her sideways. Jose wrenches her upright. He holds her there as he pulls a cloth from his pocket and wraps it around her face. She presses the cloth with her fingers. She grips the saddle with the other hand and nods to him.

"Do not look. Keep your head down."

She nods again and sinks down into the saddle. Jose leads the horses over the bodies in the road, past the bodies hanging from the trees, past the overturned army truck. The girl is quiet, she sits still and careful in the saddle, face masked in cloth.

Tom would like to be riding behind her. He would like to climb up onto the horse, he would like to slide his arms around her belly and press his face into her back and sleep. Curled around the curve of her back. Instead he sits alone and sniffs as the smell of his urine grows sweet in the heat, sweet against the horse sweat and leather. Animal, vegetable, mineral. He is turning to stone as he sits astride this horse.

They could wait until dusk, he thinks. They could wait until it is dark and it is safer. It would be best for all of them. They are in a state of shock. Consider the girl, in her condition—it would be better to wait. This heat, and this smell. As it is the girl is not moving, she is sitting perfectly still and letting the horse carry her through the village massacre.

He acknowledges that they now have the morphine. He knows that he is still alive, more or less. But he has paid a price. He would like to unsee what he has seen but he already knows that is not possible. He has made his acquaintance with the contingent world, he knows now that it is a place built of madness. Past the farm there lies nothing at all. It unfolds and extends without reason. He, who has seen so little, can now see future's history, that is going to happen in this country.

There is no life for him there. The last of his illusions slipping away. Jose says to them that they must continue. He says they cannot afford to wait until dusk. The girl, her face muffled by the cloth, does not respond. Tom is also silent. They will continue. They will go back to the farm. But it is like he has left a limb in the village, a hand or a leg or a foot. The world he has believed in has gone. It is lying by the side of the road in a puddle of blood. Therefore he is no longer innocent; his fetishes have been taken away.

WHEN THE THREE approach the farm, it is morning, or nearly morning. The girl sits bolt upright, having removed the cloth from her face and gripped the reins, which now drape over

171

her belly. She stares into darkness, into the night, as they ride down the back roads.

For a long time she believed there was security in land, but now she sees there is no place with land in the country, she understands the land is receding from them all. Without property, the terrain becomes senseless. The country becomes a maze, the landscape now unrecognizable, the markers slipping away. And she is moving in widening circles, she is trapped inside a growing labyrinth.

As if there is only the farm (although it is shrinking). And there are only these men (although they are fading). She could travel the country and she would always end up back where she had started. It was not entirely as she had seen it to be. Around her the country splinters and fragments. There are deep shudders of violence while inside her the baby grows, shrinking the world down as it does. Without the baby things would be different. Without the baby she would be free.

But she is not free. None of them are. Such a thing no longer exists in the country. Instead they are retreating to the relative quiet of the valley. They have never crossed the land so quickly. Two whites and a native—a bad combination, at a time when whites and natives alike are being shot down. They are running for their lives and that is no metaphor. It is no longer the time for metaphor in the country, the girl thinks. Now there is only the thing itself.

When they come upon the farm in the morning it looks the same. The farm is quiet and the valley is empty. The rebellion has not yet arrived. They are safe. They are on their own land—land that is theirs, temporarily, they remind themselves that everything is now temporary, including and especially the land. But the farm, the property, still has its effect. False though it may be. They feel the chaos begin to recede before they are through the gate.

They stable the horses and Tom clutches the canvas bag with the morphine. He is exhausted and sleepless. His memories of the land in turmoil merge with fragments of the old man: the fits of pain, the medicine running low, the eyes crawling the ceiling and wall. The old man is the last surviving link to the old world, the old order, that they have recently seen crumbling. He is the last collection and already a ruin, but Tom reminds himself that he has the morphine, that at least here there is something yet he can do.

He starts walking up the drive to the house. Jose and the girl follow and together they enter. Where there is death throughout. They have been surrounded by death at top speed and now—now they are in the midst of death in slow motion, death that is slow as treacle. It is something different but no less gruesome. The house is filled with its smell: like all the doors and windows have been kept shut for the sole purpose of keeping the stink trapped inside.

Celeste runs to the door and pushes them back outside.

"Low. Keep your voices low."

Although they were saying nothing. Although they were completely silent. Her face is stricken and in it all is there to see. She proceeds to tell them anyway.

That the past thirty-six hours have been very bad. All day

he was in pain and screaming for the pills. She fed them to him, she kept feeding him pills until the pain was gone and he could rest. Then the pills wore off and then she heard thumps and pounding and she ran to his room and he was there, thrashing in the bed, screaming in agony, hitting his head against the wall and headboard, and she fed him more pills.

At nightfall he went mute. He opened his mouth but his voice was gone. His tongue flap-flapped in the air but no sound came out. She stood by the side of the bed. He motioned with his hand for more pills. She told him she had no more. He motioned for the pills again. She asked if he would like some water, some soup, some milk. If he would like her to rub his feet. He opened his mouth but could not scream.

She is glad that they are back. She is very glad. Tom nods and swallows.

"Is he sleeping? How is he now?"

"He is no longer himself."

"I will go and see him."

"Yes."

He hands her the canvas bag.

"There is medicine in there."

Jose takes the bag from Celeste and looks at Tom.

"You should sit down and recover from the journey. I will give him the morphine."

He disappears. Now Celeste leads them, Tom and the pregnant girl, into the kitchen. She makes them sit down, she boils some water for tea.

"The old man is no longer himself. You must be prepared."

"I am sorry we left you alone."

Celeste makes a cup of tea and Tom drinks it. She finds a piece of cake and brings it to him. Celeste, who does not seem surprised to see the girl, offers her a piece. The girl refuses. She lets the cup of tea cool in front of her. Celeste sits down and eats the girl's slice of cake. Tom takes a bite of the cake. His eyes are vacant.

The girl watches him. She sees how much he has been changed. She raises the cup of tea to her lips and then abruptly drops it back into the saucer. She stands and leaves the kitchen. She is not going to wait any longer. Whatever has to be faced will be faced now. After all, what does it matter to her—what is the old man to her, what is this place, this boy and this woman, what do they matter to her, of all people—

She goes into the bedroom and it is more or less like a wall swinging into her face and then she remembers. She actually flinches at the sight. Tom comes rushing down the hall behind her and it is too late—she cannot go running, she cannot back out or tell him not to enter, he is literally blocking the door behind her. There is no way to go but forward and so they enter the room together.

And yes. They are aghast. The old man lies on the bed and more than ever he secretes the toxic charisma of the dying. He sprays the air with it like a cat. They cannot look away. They stare instead at the limbs that have collapsed, the face that has gone yellow, the shallow mounds beneath the bed sheets that are now the old man—they are pretty damn sure he is dying at last.

175

It is plain as anything. The reality of the dying and the reality of the larger situation. Which is equally dire. There is no way around it. The old man is dying and the farm will die with him. Tom has run out of time. He has been running out of time for days and weeks. He is a fool. The world outside is beyond all control but the man in front of him—he sees the body stretched out before him and knows there will never be the time to say, what was it he intended to say? What would he have said, if he had found the time?

He does not know, that is part of the problem. He is crying. The girl is dry-eyed and passes Tom a handkerchief. She tells him to blow his nose and get a grip. He takes the handkerchief and blows his nose. He gives the handkerchief back to the girl but still does not have a grip on the situation. And the girl needs him to hurry up, she needs him to pull himself together, because as it is he is not helping.

The two of them and the world outside and the old man in the bed. The old man, who has lost the power of speech and no longer retains the power of movement, whose limbs lie frozen—the old man is glaring at Tom. It is not their imagination. The old man has had enough. The old man is dying and he is not happy about it. When he glares at Tom it is not a trick of the dying physiognomy. It is the absolute truth of what he is feeling.

It is therefore too much for Tom. Who will never be able to say what he feels. Who would gladly trade ten years of his own life for one of his father's, for another month, another week or day or hour, but who knows such transactions are impossible.

The feeling, his willingness, has never had anywhere to go, and now more than ever he does not know where to put it. Pressing his hands to hide his face, his body heavy with this deadlock, Tom leaves the room.

The girl closes the door behind him. She goes to the side of the bed. She stares down at the old man, dry-eyed. He glares back up at her, dry-eyed. They remain like this until the old man's eyes empty and his head falls back into the pillow. He closes his eyes. The girl places her palm on his forehead, she grips his wrist between her fingers. He has slipped away again.

She adjusts the covers. She thinks, You wanted to die here and you did not even know that you were dying. You wanted to come home and die. That is more than what they got. The men and women and children who were hacked to their deaths. Also the soldiers. Also the un-soldiers. And now I am here, too, and I am backed into a corner but at least I am still living. Me and the one inside me. For what that is worth.

Not much, she thinks. It is not worth very much. She lets go of the cover. She turns and leaves the room. She does not want to see Tom or the others so she wanders the halls instead. For lack of anything better to do. She enters the wings that have been closed for months. She leaves the zone of dying where they have been sequestered all these weeks. She walks through the wings (closed but not locked). She opens doors and passes through corridors.

Here she finds rooms emptied of their contents. The walls are masked with sheets of plastic and white cloth. She can barely recognize it as the house she used to know. She looks and sees. Here is the room where this happened. Here is the hall where that happened. It looks nothing like what it once was. It looks like it is all ending. Like it has already ended and they are as extraneous as ghosts.

They and everything that happened to them in this place. It is being spirited away. It is not yet past. But it is slipping away. She can see that soon there will be no way of talking about it. That the past is going to be sealed off and the keys to the locks will be lost. It is already happening and she is starting to forget, she has already forgotten, how she got to where she now is.

There is so much empty floor. Once she was drowning in society, suffocating in its antechambers. Now it receded like ice melting in water. She looks up. These vaulted ceilings, these stone floors, these bay windows and chandeliers. It is too good to let go and too good to destroy. They will make it a government building. A department store. A post office or a bank. They will fill the rooms again and the people will talk about the architecture. They will say it is a good relic of the past preserved. It is a question, she believes, of time. Whether it is one year or one decade or one month.

The girl is sitting huddled and cold in the corner of an empty room when she hears the voices. They are both hushed and panicked. She hears a word here and there, following the native dialect with difficulty. She listens closer, concentrating, and hears more:

"We cannot stay any longer."

"Look around you. He is dying, it is a matter of days."

"We have run out of time. You do not know how bad it has become. It is spreading like an infection."

"That is just the mood. It will not last. You will see that it will not last."

"Listen. They will kill us. It is not just the settlers. They are killing loyalists all across the country. They are making examples of people. And you are a loyalist if you do not take the oath, it has become like that."

The voices subside. The girl leans her head back and closes her eyes. She is nearly asleep when the voices return:

"I am no loyalist."

"You went out in search of adventure. Like a child."

"If I was looking for adventure I would have joined the Oath Takers."

"But you do not like them."

"No."

"I do not like them either. I am waiting for something else for this country."

A short laugh.

"You will die waiting. There is nothing else. It is a miracle that even this has happened. We are surrounded by a miracle."

"It is not my miracle."

"You do not have any choice. That is what I am trying to tell you. The choice has been made for us. We must do what is best. In order to survive."

"He is your father. How can you speak like this?"

"He has been no father to me."

"You know nothing. He has tried."

"That means nothing. He has given me nothing."

"He has given you a home. That is the love he could offer us."

"He gave me the same home he would have given any native, any slave who worked his land. And you call this his love—"

A choked cry.

"No, no. I will not be sorry when he dies."

Their voices move down the corridor. The girl peers into the darkness. She hears nothing further but she understands. The ghostly echo between Tom and Jose. Jose, who is so much like the old man and therefore so much like her. More— Jose's hatred for Tom and his ignorance, the things Tom had been protected from knowing. Tom who knows nothing and Jose who sees everything. The father's strange patrimony.

The secrets of this place. No wonder Jose and Celeste stayed when the others had gone. The old man meaning something to them yet. She cannot believe that she did not see it earlier. Nevertheless, it had been madness for them to stay. She wonders that Jose, canny as he is, could have made this error. It is true none of them know how far the rebellion will spread. But there is little margin for error, and none for human sentiment.

Eventually, she falls asleep. She lies huddled in the corner, on the floor, for hours. When she wakes it is with a jolt to the sound of footsteps. Her sleep has been crammed with the fragments of bad things—the volcano, the veranda, the dying fish. She gets up and half expects that this is the end, for her belly to be slit open and her head sliced off. She wakes out of the dream and she hears the voices again, she hears Tom and Celeste and is temporarily reassured.

She labors to her feet and walks in the direction of the voices. She goes into the old man's bedroom. He lies spread-eagled on the bed, body flailing from side to side. His eyes roll in circles and there is froth gathering around his mouth. Celeste is asking where the pills are. The girl tells her there's no point. No way he can swallow anything—just look at him. Celeste insists. The pills. Where are the pills?

She tells Celeste that Tom has them. She does not know where they are. Tom has all the morphine. Where is Tom? She does not know where Tom has gone. The girl cannot take her eyes off the old man. He is panting for breath, he claws at the bed sheets, at his chest and neck, at the air in front of his mouth. He screams in silence, his eyes yellow and bulging with rage and agony.

She steps forward—as Celeste continues to ask for the pills, again and again—and she grabs the old man's hand. And even though his body keeps convulsing his arm, at least, is still. She grips it tight and tells him that it is going to be okay. It is going to be okay. She holds tighter and then he jerks his head to her, eyes staring. And she tells him again that it is going to be okay and he nods. He is a man grasping at straws and she can see in his eyes that he wants to believe her.

Yes. It is going to be okay. How okay and what okay she doesn't know but she keeps telling him. It is going to be okay. And he looks at her and then he nods. Yes. It will. Will it? And then Celeste plunges a needle into his arm and they hear the quick suck of the syringe and he collapses back onto the bed.

The girl looks up. Celeste puts the needle down on the bedside table. She rolls the old man onto his side and with a quick jerk pulls down his pants. The girl looks at the old man's face—it is frozen, it has no expression beyond resigned outrage. Celeste taps the morphine pills out of the bottle and shoves them up his ass. Her face says nothing as she pulls the old man's trousers up again and lowers him to the bed. She pulls the covers up and he lies in perfect stillness.

Tom stands in the doorway, gripping the open canvas medicine bag to his chest. Celeste sighs and steps back from the bed. The girl stares at her blankly.

"Is he alive?"

The three of them stare at each other and then Celeste leaves the room. She is conscious of having done more than she intended. There is a long low wheeze and then the smell of shit fills the room. Like nothing they have ever smelled. The girl knows they should clean him but it is a distant thought. Tom shuffles up to the side of the bed and stares down at the old man's face.

"What did Celeste give him?"

Carine shakes her head and walks to the door. Tom finds a chair and sits down. She looks back at him.

"What are you doing?"

"We can't leave him."

She thinks about it. She needs to lie down. She needs to eat. She cannot even breathe in this room. Tom is looking up at her. He is sitting in the cloud of smell and his face is full of decision, it says he is going to sit, for as long as it takes. After all, it is all that he has left. She nods.

"Fine."

She leaves the room.

12

The old man stays in a coma for the next three days. He does not stir. His breath is regular as a clock but a clock that is gradually slowing. They listen to his breath and now they are waiting for him to die in earnest. To go on and get it over with. His breath is slowing but too slowly for their taste.

They would like him to die. They cannot wait much longer—they do not believe it is physically possible. The strain is immense. They are not getting enough sleep. They are not remembering to eat. Celeste is cooking all day. Always there is a pot on the stove, she is cooking through their last remaining store of food. But they have lost their appetite.

They are the living and it is difficult for the living to contend with the dying. There is not enough space. The old man inflates and expands and he presses them against the walls of the house. They are having trouble breathing from this position. While the old man's own breath swishes rhythmically in and out.

Flattened against the walls and ceiling they listen to the

sound of his breathing. They wait for the walls to crack. For the house to collapse. It is obvious the structure cannot hold. There is not room for all of them and the dying and something will have to give. They hope it will be the house and not them. That it will not be their lungs that collapse first.

Tom alone sits by the old man's bed and holds his vigil. He does not want the old man to lie unattended. He does not want him to die alone. Of course it is a possibility. He might get up to stretch his legs or use the toilet and *whoosh* in a flash he may go. It could end like this, it is a roll of the dice each time. But Tom needs to believe that there are still things he can do. At least inside this one room. That some things can still be maintained, even if too late.

Therefore Tom sits by the bed and the others, they sit pressed against the wall, they tumble out windows and crawl back in again. For three days Tom sits. He is persistent. He will not allow a single second of the dying to escape him. The others watch and to them it is like he is grasping the dying man to him, like he would devour the already stinking body if he could. He has the sense that he will dissolve when the old man dies, he can see the moment around the corner.

But even Tom's persistence cracks in the face of this interminable dying. On the third day he leaves the bedroom and goes outside. He has had nothing but the smell of dying. The sweetness of which is now as strong as candy boiling. Lately he is having trouble breathing, he pinches his nose and holds his breath when he leans in to lift his father, to wipe him down and change the diaper.

The shit has the color and consistency of tar. A smear of tar on white muslin. Each time Tom examines the diaper like he is reading runes. Like there are signs written into the excrement.

Tom sits in the dark on the porch steps. He remembers putting the outdoor furniture into storage all those months ago. It goes without saying that it feels like a lifetime earlier. He looks down to the river, which is now running clear. Nine months—it has taken nine months but at last the river is clear. There have been no further signs of the rebellion in the valley. There has been nothing but the deafening silence of the old man's death.

Later, Jose comes out and joins him. He leans against one of the pillars and lights a cigarette. Tom speaks without looking at him.

"Do you think they are coming?"

"I do not know."

Tom nods. He continues to stare at the river. Which is not only clean but also flowing. In which there are fish, even if they are not huge in number and not yet breeding.

"I will give them everything. Our thousand acres. They can take the house—I have no need of it. I can live on an acre. I can live on less. Only—"

"Only you do not want to die."

"No. I do not want to die."

"I do not think they will come so far. There is nothing in it for them. They will return to the city and make their de-mands. Their leader will make a deal with the Government like before. They are not mindless and they are not without purpose."

He is watching Tom as he says this. Tom shivers.

"I do not want to die."

"Nor I."

Jose turns and goes into the house. Tom stays on the porch. The air is clean and warm. It will be summer in no time. If the old man does not die by summer his body will rot in the heat and that will be that. It will end in this way. It is hard to believe the old man will die. It seems more likely that he will rot before their gathered eyes, it seems more likely he will stay with them forever, undead as he now is.

Tom stands up and goes inside the house. In the kitchen, Celeste has left a tray of cold food. Tom thinks he will take it to the girl, who is sitting with the old man. He takes the tray and goes into the bedroom. The old man's body has not changed. It is still churning through the air like a wind machine. One of the lids has gone up. The white of the eye is visible and the pupil stares at nothing.

Tom puts the tray down. He lifts and then presses the lid down and sits down. The girl nods to him. They are neither enemies nor friends. It has gone beyond that kind of thing. They may as well be the last two people left in the world. Why did you lift his eye like that? Forget it, she shakes her head. She is tired, she sits by the old man's feet. She presses her eyes with the heel of her hand.

She stands and leaves the room. Tom stares at the old man. In the last day there has been a change and he has been weighted to the bed. He can see the change clearly. Like there are a thousand stones resting on his body. The old man has been transformed by death's alchemy: he had been weightless and brittle, now his body is heavy and dense like lead. Tom can no longer move him; his father can no longer be stirred.

He is also now a noise machine. His breath creaks in and out of his body. Like he has a bellows packed inside him. Like he is a giant bagpipe tucked into the bed. His body is very loud despite the stillness, it is making more noise than it made in all its life. Tom sits by the side of the bed and eventually falls asleep. He is dozing, he is slumbering, to the noise of his father dying.

HE WAKES TO a sudden and broad silence. In panic, he leans close to the bed. His breath—certainly his breath has slowed. Tom pitches his body to the bed and puts his ear against his father's mouth. A long silence. So long that Tom's heart rate rises in the quiet. It bangs against his chest. Then a sharp intake of breath that is dry—very dry, more like a mechanical click than a breath. Then another long silence.

A swell of nausea rises inside him. He leans closer to the old man. He listens to the silence. He counts it out—one, two, three—ten seconds, more like twelve. Fifteen. Can he be dead? Is this how it looks? He places his fingers on his neck and searches for a pulse. The vein is still and he presses harder and harder until he is almost throttling him with his hands. He feels nothing, no whisper of a pulse. And yet the old man does not look dead.

It has been thirty seconds—it has been longer, he has lost track. He freezes with his hands on the old man's neck. His head is spinning. He tries to recover his count. He loosens his grip and drops his hands. He clenches them together in his lap. To keep himself from grabbing the old man's neck again. Please. Do not go. Now he wishes he knew how to pray. A sound as loud as a shotgun bursts out of the old man's throat and Tom sees his body finally let go.

Tom sits by the side of the bed. For a long time his mind is blank. He stares down at the corpse. He reaches for his arm and then stops. He does not move. The old man's face grows rigid. It happens in a minute. One minute or maybe two. He is human and then he is no longer human, he is a thing with its mouth open like a maw. Its eyes staring in shock at the ceiling. Its eyes having opened at some point in its death.

It is not a face for the dying. It turns out the face of death is not a face for the dead. Sickened by what he sees, Tom tries to close the jaw. He presses and presses and the open maw does not yield until he uses the heel of his palm and the knuckles of his fist and then with a snap the mouth closes. He reaches forward and presses hard on the lids, until he feels the old man's eyes sink beneath his fingers.

Tom drops his hands. He stands for a moment and then quickly leaves the room. He passes the kitchen, he can hear Celeste working at the stove. It is the middle of the night but she is banging pots and pans—she is unhappy with him and

Jose, it is like when they were children. Now the old man is dead and who knows what will happen, what she will do with her dissatisfaction. Tom does not go into the kitchen. He goes to his room and gets into bed.

He does not actually sleep. He sits beneath the covers and stares into darkness. The old man's death lying huddled in the corner of his brain. Whether it is dormant or expired he does not know. But it is quiet and the rest of his brain is like a desert or wasteland. It is like he has been emptied. He is not capable of stirring the death in his mind. He imagines that blankness is preferable.

Eventually, he exits the house and discovers it is dawn. Light appears on the horizon and he sees that the soil is green and the land stretches out in the direction of the sun. The land has been liberated. Its imprimatur is gone. Tom is in a daze. I will be in a daze for a long time, he thinks. That is the first thought that he has in relation to the old man's death. A pop as he is set free. Then his mind is quiet again.

Past the gate he sees the girl, sitting underneath a tree. She is staring down the track. It is morning and getting warm. Tom thinks: she is going to run. She has done it before and there is nothing to stop her doing it again. He will tell her that the old man is dead and then there will be no reason for her to stay. They should both leave. There is no point in staying. But Tom does not think that he can leave, he does not think he is able.

He sits down next to her and she does not look up. They sit side by side. He sits and does not think he will ever be able to stand up again.

After a long silence, he speaks.

"Are you going to leave?"

She shakes her head.

"Are you thinking about it?"

She shakes her head again.

He nods and turns back to the road. He does not tell her the old man is dead. He tells himself that there is time for that later. He tells himself that there is time for many things, that one day he will love the memory as he never loved the man, one day he will be able to do this. But he does not see how such a thing will come to pass, the hope of ordinary things having grown impossible. Meanwhile, the death still prone inside him.

The girl came down to the road in order to escape the house. When she reached the gate and saw the dirt road— then she thought about going. She thought she should go now, while the road was open, while the country was quiet. There was nothing here worth waiting for. She did not believe in the farm's safety. But then she had another instinct and changed her mind. Soon. But not yet. She sat down beneath the tree instead.

Now she looks at Tom. His heart quickens. He stares at the ground and says nothing. She reaches out and gently strokes his hair.

"I said to Jose that I would help tend the garden."

He nods.

"We can grow things to eat. He said that he would show me."

He does not move but waits. She strokes his hair again and

then she tells him that she will stay. She tells him that she is not going to go. She knows that Tom will never leave the farm. The truth is that she does not mind lying. She drops her hand back down to her belly. She feels it hard beneath her fingers and then her mouth goes dry. When she speaks it is without meaning to.

"He is not going to come."

Tom looks up.

"Who?"

She ignores him and presses harder on her belly. She tries to press her fingers in. Her body has changed. The baby made of lead has turned her torso into wood. She cannot break or crack it. She tries. She makes a fist and sinks her knuckles in but it does not give or even splinter. It is hard as the polished surface of a table and solid throughout.

She shakes her head and looks at Tom.

"It is made of wood. It has turned into wood."

How can she make him understand? He does not know what to say, he does not even know what she means. He has no way of responding. She reaches out and takes his hand and lays it on her belly. She tries to show him what has happened.

"Do you see? It is made of wood. I am turning into wood."

It is solid as rock. He starts to think he understands what she means. But then there is a stirring. A kick of alien life. The lead baby stirring. They look at each other.

"Do you see?"

She says it again. Her eyes are hard. She thinks to herself that it is hopeless. She will never be able to leave. She will be stuck dragging her wood belly back and forth across the length of the farm forever. It will kill her in the end. She asks him again. If he sees, if he can understand how it happened, how her belly turned to wood. He nods. He almost thinks he does see but of course does not.

They give up and stop talking. The girl sits and presses her hands into her wood belly. The wood begins to hum and vibrate. She turns pale. Tom does not feel the vibration. He is too busy staring down the road. He sees a cloud of dust. The sound of a motor in the distance. He sits up and peers across to the horizon.

With a roar an army truck catapults into view. The earth now trembling. The dust scattering in plumes behind the vehicle. A group of men hang out the side, holding machetes and AK-47s. The car careens across the road and the machetes swing. The girl lets out a strangled cry. Tom pulls her to her feet and together they crouch behind the tree.

The army truck continues to race forward. From the opposite direction, a horse and rider appear on the road, coming from the direction of the stables, heading toward the truck. It is Jose, who does not realize about the men. Who is about to make a terrible mistake. Tom almost cries out a warning but quickly the girl presses her hand against his mouth.

They watch as the horse moves down the road, the roaring vehicle and the galloping animal pulled together across the horizon. The truck now clearly in view. Tom waits for Jose to turn around, to veer and to run. He does not. He rides straight up to the truck and comes to a halt before the men. The horse snorting and rearing as the truck engine idles. Horrified, Tom waits for the gunshot.

There is no gunshot. Jose points in the direction of the house. He says something to the men. A second later he is continuing down the road. The men shout something and he raises his arm in reply, then disappears down the track. The men give another cry. They gun the motor and the truck leaps forward. In the direction of the house. In the direction of where they are sitting. The wheels spinning through the dirt.

Tom stares at the vehicle. The truck now lifting off the ground as it races toward them. The girl reaches for his hand and grips it. Tears streaming down her face. It is too late, Tom thinks. It is too late. His knuckles white and shaking. He watches the truck and braces himself for what is coming. They both do.

They sit by the tree and wait.

acknowledgments

Thank you to Ellen Levine, Clare Conville, Millicent Bennett, Dominick Anfuso, Martha Levin, Chloe Perkins, Meghan O'Rourke, Sophie Fiennes, Harland Miller, Geraldine Ogilvy, and Hari Kunzru.